80 Days of Pleasure

AIKEN PONDER

Words to Ponder Publishing
Chagrin Falls, Ohio

80 Days of Pleasure by Aiken Ponder

Address inquiries to Words to Ponder Publishing Company, LLC

Trade Paperback ISBN 978-1-7358795-9-8
Ebook ISBN 978-1-941328-56-9

Words to Ponder Publishing Company, LLC
Printed in the United States of America
For more information, visit https://www.florenza.org or
https://www.wordstoponderpublishing.com.

Text copyright @ 2021 by Words to Ponder Publishing Company, LLC
Cover Design by J. L. Woodson for Woodson Creative Studio.
Interior Design by Lissa Woodson for Woodson Creative Studio

♦ DEDICATION ♦

I dedicate this book to my husband, best friend, and soulmate, my Papa Bear. To my children, Jessica and Missy who are my first and loudest cheerleaders. To family and friends, who are my most incredible supporters. To Naleighna Kai and the NK Tribe Called Success for taking me under your wing and teaching this bird to soar. To Stephanie M. Freeman, my "drink and two-step" partner in crime.

To my editor, Naleighna Kai, who takes the broken pieces of my words ensuring they are woven together in such a fashion, they create a beautiful tapestry. To the beta readers who dedicate countless hours to be the first set of eyes to partake of the deliciousness of this story.

And to you, the reader, for your encouragement and support of the beautiful gift of writing given to me from God.

Prologue

Sarvanti's long-toned legs glistened in the sun as she trotted across the parking lot towards the Buick Cascada. The oversized khaki shorts did little to hide curves that only youth, clean eating, and hours in the gym could create. Although Sarvanti's stunning and statuesque features easily could have landed her on the cover of any fashion magazine, she loved working as a valet. Sarvanti quickly slid her lean frame behind the wheel of luxury cars that many of her male classmates only lied about driving.

Being outside in the fresh air was far better than being cooped up behind a desk, fake smiling at customers while answering phones any day. Just the thought of being trapped in a windowless cubical caused her temples to throb. Singers, athletes, actors, politicians, and such. She learned that if she kept her looks natural, not drawing too much attention to herself, she could get up close and personal. As a journalist student, the stories she overheard could easily make her rich and famous. For right now, she was just a fly on a wall with a very thick notebook.

The lush black leather interior was a stark contrast to the white exterior. The car gleamed from a recent detail and professional waxing.

"Who did you meet today, Vanti?" Her mother's thick Italian accent echoed through her Bluetooth earpiece. She was fascinated with those who achieved the American Dream and always wanted to know which celebrity her daughter rubbed elbows with.

"Someone you'd just die to meet." Sarvanti teased while glancing over her shoulder, ensuring no one was within earshot. "But you'd think with his fame, he'd be endorsed by Mercedes or Maserati."

"Endorsed? He must be very famous? What type of vehicle does he have?" Her mother's voice rose an octave higher. Next to celebrities, she loved automobiles more.

"He's someone you've always wanted to meet," she said. "I can afford this on my salary." Sarvanti spoke into her earpiece as she hit the key fob. Cell phones were not permitted at work, especially while driving.

"If it's who I think it is, please take a photo for me," her mother pleaded in her ear.

"I'm not supposed to, but …" she said as she opened the car door. "I'll try." She glanced around again. "You know I'm not supposed to ask customers for their autographs—" Sarvanti put her foot on the brake pedal then punched the start button. "Besides, he's not alone. He's with a young girl. Maybe it's another one of those charity things he does. You know, take an orphan to lunch or something. Only there are no paparazzi."

"Just try."

"Alright, but if I get fired," she warned. "I'll be moving back in with you. Love you, mom." She tapped her ear, ending the call as she drove the few hundred feet back to the front door.

* * *

"Thank you again for lunch. You didn't have to bring me to such a fancy place." Nova nervously rolled her thumbs together as she looked down at a pair of scuffed shoes and holes forming at the knees of her jeans. She glanced at his plate. "How was the—what's it called again?"

"Cioppino, and it was delicious once they prepared it correctly."

"Well, you sent it back six times," she said, then suddenly added, "I'm sorry. I wasn't trying to be disrespectful. I'd just be scared they'd try to mess with my food afterward."

"You'll learn. You must demand perfection, especially when you're paying. I'm the customer. They're here to serve me." He squared his shoulders and tilted his chin forward. "Besides, I like the way they prepare the shrimp, clams, and mussels. Sending it back prompted them to get their act together." He pushed his dish forward. "You look as if you really enjoyed your meal."

Her eyes cast downward as the heat rose to her cheeks. They matched the carnations in the miniature vase of water on the table. Her plate bore no signs that a healthy portion of lasagna had occupied it a few moments before. The dish that held the crème Brule was even cleaner. Both plates looked as though they had been licked clean. Truthfully, if seated alone, she probably would have. "I would've been happy with either McDonald's or Wendy's. You didn't have to spend so much."

"Nonsense," he said, placing a platinum credit card back into the wallet, then took out cash instead as he stood. "How would it look if I took you to a fast-food greasy burger joint?" He walked around and pulled her chair back, allowing her to stand.

The waitress partially opened the black leather folder with the bills. Her face contorted as she lifted the slip of paper and glanced under it. She mumbled as she slapped the binder closed then turned to walk away.

Pausing, he reached into his pocket, revealing a necklace which he placed around her neck.

She immediately reached up to grasp the small diamond dangling from her throat.

"It isn't fancy," he said. "I didn't want to draw attention to it."

Tears filled her eyes. "It's beautiful."

"Just a little something to remind you I'm always thinking of you." Nova leaned into his hug. Although only thirteen, she was very tall for her age. The top of her head practically reached his shoulder as they walked side by side towards the front door.

"Each place seems to get nicer than the one before," she said softly.

"I don't want you to think I'm trynna get stuff from you … I mean, I still can't believe that after all this time, you found me." Tears formed in the inner corners of her eyes. She quickly reached up with a hand and swiped them away. "All my life, I was told no one knew who my dad was." She watched as the valet drove the white convertible towards them. "When my mom died from an overdose of heroin, I went from one home to another home …."

Placing his hand on her chin and tilting her face towards his, "I can only imagine all that you've gone through, and I'm so sorry," he said. "I'm here now, and I'm not going anywhere."

"Some of the things I've gone through were—"

"You don't have to say them. I just need you to have a bit more patience. My assistants are working on getting your documentation in order. It'll all be worth the wait, I promise." He smiled broadly, and it put her at ease. "Did you know I gave you your name?"

"You did?"

He kissed her forehead. "Yes, because I knew instantly, you'd be a star."

"My life is no movie unless you are looking for a horror flick."

Nova closed her eyes, rocking on her heels. The sound of his voice alone was like music to her ears. The lyrics were foreign, and she didn't even care that she didn't know the words. If this was a dream, she didn't ever want to wake up. "Do you mind if I call you daddy?"

As soon as the car came to a stop, he held the door open as she slid behind the passenger seat. "Not at all. As a matter of fact, I insist that you do."

He walked around to the awaiting valet as she held open the door with one hand and her palm out with the other. His six-foot-seven-inch frame instantly filled the entire driver's seat. He pulled the door closed without so much as a thank you or tip. The valet's mouth was still ajar as the car sped off and entered traffic.

Nova glanced in the side mirror, and several flashes nearly blinded her. "People take a lot of photos of you," she said.

"I hate when they do that." He scowled, but it quickly disappeared. "I once snatched someone's phone and threw it to the ground." His head went backward as he laughed. "You should have seen his face when the heel of my shoe smashed the phone. It was priceless."

"But—" Nova thought better than saying anything else. In an article in G-Q Magazine, she'd once read that he welcomed fans asking for autographs and photos. Something about his tone made her keep the thoughts to herself.

"Don't believe everything you read," he snapped as though he had read her mind. Then added in a softer tone, "I like my privacy."

* * *

"Thank you for that enthusiastic round of applause," Mayor Swinson bellowed into the microphone. His broad smile caused his beady brown eyes to become practically invisible behind his full cheeks. "Like you, I too am excited about our visitors and the wonderful program they have begun in our fine city." Cheers and loud clapping erupted again. The mayor joined in by pumping his fist in the air. He then raised his hands, asking everyone to kindly be seated.

"Today, we welcome Dallas Avery and his teammates." Dallas' large palm came down on the mayor's right shoulder, nearly engulfing it completely. "They, along with members of the police, clergy, and national and international corporations, have combined efforts to stop human trafficking. It is my greatest honor to ban together with this wonderful organization." Mayor Swinson stepped to his right as Dallas began speaking into the microphone.

"We're so very honored to be here and to share information regarding our organization, A Place to Ponder. To provide a haven for those trapped in human trafficking, we've partnered with local, international, private, and public entities with one purpose in mind, to protect those who cannot help themselves." He looked to his left, "Adrian Hernandez has more information to share." Dallas stepped to the right of the podium.

"Thank you, Mayor Swinson, my teammates, and you for joining us this afternoon. We're very excited to have a special group of youngsters selected via lottery to attend the *Banquet with a Ball Player* yearly event. Each of them will have the opportunity to sit down and eat with several of us and share their story." He applauded in their direction. One teen with braids and a toothy grin waved enthusiastically. "Every year, millions of vulnerable children and women are trafficked for sex around the world. The perpetrator hunts for those who're most vulnerable and then cunningly gains the victim's trust. The nightmare of sex trafficking thrives when law enforcement cannot or does not protect vulnerable children and women." Heads nodded, some women in the audience gasped. "Together with law enforcement, we aim to make it difficult for these punks to profit from selling children and adults caught in their traps. They will know we are hot on their trails."

Cheers and applause erupted from the audience.

Chapter 1

Plano, Texas

Alicia's thighs tingled as she relived the first night in his arms.

She stretched muscular cocoa arms above her head then slowly opened her hazel green eyes as the meticulously designed room came into focus.

Alicia had expected his condo to be an overly masculine crash-pad complete with dozens of "I love me" awards. Or that it would have a pool table in the living room, a tiger on a gold chain, and massive television sets mounted on every wall. She had been pleasantly surprised the moment she crossed the threshold.

Dallas was not only incredible on the basketball court; he was also a man of purpose. After some encouragement and with a bit of assistance from her, his condo went from tasteful to stellar. Exquisite décor, rich fabrics, luscious colors, elegant artwork, and sensual elements now greeted guests upon arrival. The massive condo displayed sophistication. By far, her favorite feature was the redbrick fireplace positioned so perfectly that the flames reflected beautifully off the cathedral windows. They instantly whisked her away to faraway lands where knights slew dragons with golden swords.

Alicia shifted the pillows behind her back. A slight smirk crept over her full lips. *It's been over eleven weeks, and you're still waking up in this man's bed.* She shook her head as if to silence the accusatory tone of her inner thoughts. *I blame it on these damn Signature sheets.* She tugged the exotic cotton topper around her neck.

Or the fact that he gave you your first orgasm. An inner voice retorted.

"Speaking of eleven—"

"Are you talking to yourself?" Dallas walked into the bedroom holding a silver tray with a lead-crystal glass filled with freshly squeezed orange juice, a slice of multigrain toast, and a bowl of mixed fruit.

She playfully batted her long eyelashes. "Who me?" She placed a palm alongside her collarbone. "Of course not."

He positioned the tray across Alicia's lap, kissed her forehead then reclaimed the spot next to her between the sheets.

"How sweet. Breakfast in bed," Alicia gushed.

"I thought you'd be a bit famished after our workout last night," Dallas said with a husky voice which caused Alicia to tremble with appreciation. "Are you cold?" he asked, rubbing her forearms with his hands.

"Far from it." A slight moan escaped as she bit down softly on her bottom lip.

He traced an invisible mustache with both hands. "Oh, so you want some more of this?" he said. "And here it is, I thought you were worn out …."

She laughed while playfully flicking his arm then placed the tray and contents onto the floor. "Oh, I see that halo is starting to tilt." She laughed. "If I tried to stand, I'm certain my legs might be a bit shaky—"

Snuggling closer, he panted, "Then don't stand."

"Dallas." Was as much as she could say before his lips covered hers in a deep passionate kiss. He mounted her with a sense of familiarity that suggested they'd performed this dance a hundred times.

Each thrust caused Alicia's body to arch upward. Her legs wrapped tightly around his waist, eliciting a slight tease from Dallas. "I see those legs found strength, after all."

He reached under her buttocks and lifted her effortlessly off the mattress. Alicia's hips fit perfectly on his thighs as he slid deeper inside of her.

* * *

Dallas felt entirely at home with and inside Alicia. He'd been with other women, but none allowed him to let down his guard as she did—and it frightened him. She was the rose growing through the concrete of his heart. He gazed deeply into Alicia's eyes as his heart pounded against his chest. "Stay for just one more day, please." He had practically begged after the first night.

That was eighty nights ago.

Chapter 2

Gold Lust

"It's been nineteen hundred sixty-eight hours since you walked through my front door." Dallas moved a loc of curls behind Alicia's left ear then kissed her temple. "Tell me something that made you smile when you were a child."

Taking a few moments to ponder the question, Alicia turned towards him, then leaned on an elbow before speaking. "My grandmother gave me a jewelry box that displayed a ballerina in a pink tutu. She twirled around to music in a little circle. I used to pretend I was her and that with each twirl, I was magically transported to faraway magical lands." Alicia closed her eyes as if the imagery had flooded her memory.

"That sounds wonderful." Dallas glanced toward the ceiling as if it contained the answer. "My mother had a box that played music when it opened, but I don't think it had a dancer inside. Hers had water and dolphins painted on it."

"Mine had a castle on it." Alicia reached for her phone. "My grandmother once told me the picture was of this castle in Germany." After tapping a few keys on the iPhone, she handed the phone to Dallas. "This is actually your phone. Do you mind?"

"Not at all." Dallas entered then told her the passcode.

She typed in the website's address. "Walt Disney designed his Castle from it."

"That's nice." He swiped left through the images. "Do you still have the music box?"

"I haven't seen it in years." Alicia adjusted the pillow behind her back. "I may have given it to my brother when his daughter was returned to his care."

Dallas kicked off the cream-colored, woven jacquard down-filled duvet. "What shall we do today?"

"You mean besides this?" She flexed her hand between the two of them.

His left eyebrow arched, "Oh so now, you're Dr. Ruth." He let out a full belly laugh. "And I thought I was ensuring you'd have use of your limbs today. But if you insist." Dallas immediately rolled over to Alicia as she squirmed and laughed.

He held her steady as a quick move of his fingers opened her, revealing a warm wet core. Pausing briefly to take in her scent, he moaned in appreciation. Dallas reached off the edge of the bed and retrieved a cube of ice from the discarded glass. Tracing it along her ribcage then downward. Licking each inch of the liquid trail. Resting the cube on her mound, he waited until it all but melted. Placing the remainder of the ice on the tip of his tongue, he parted the outer folds of her core to a welcoming moan. He drank from her chalice until she dug her fingernails into the back of his neck and screamed out his name, Dallas.

Her orgasmic plateau was met with melodic moans intermingling with the erratic bumping of the headboard against the wall. Alicia's words caught in her throat as if unable to speak. He kissed a trail to her neck as he entered her. First gently, then with wicked purpose. Her body rocked with his, and together they danced a deliciously exotic kakilambe. She was entirely spent by the time he exploded in ecstasy. Her climax erupted a nanosecond afterward.

An hour later, they were under the hot water as it pulsated from the rainfall showerhead. Dallas reached for a bottle of shampoo.

"Gold Lust?" she asked, placing both hands on her ample hips.

"And repair," he added, palms out in surrender.

Dallas inhaled deeply as scents of pineapples, argon oil, passion fruit, and maracuja filled the shower and invaded her senses. "May I?" he asked.

Alicia turned then tilted her head backward, allowing Dallas's fingers to go to work on her scalp. Tingling sensations started at the nape of her neck and went all the way down to her toes, nearly causing her knees to buckle. She reached out using her left hand to grip the railing in the shower to prevent a fall. In all her life, she'd never had a man to wash her hair, let alone in the shower. The feeling of vulnerability was intoxicating.

On the court, Dallas was a beast, but not with her. He was protective without being possessive, caring and considerate, gentle and giving. At that moment, she was the recipient of his affection, and she craved more.

* * *

Dallas' cell phone rang. He ignored it the first few attempts, but with a grimace on his lips, he reached for the plush bath sheet and stepped out before she did. While drying his hair, he hit the speaker key, "What's up, Hernandez. How're you feeling, my man?" He tilted his head towards the door, signaling to Alicia he'd take the call in the bedroom.

Adrian Hernandez rapid-fire questions echoed through the speaker of the iPhone.

"Wait, slow down. I can't understand a word you're saying." Dallas sat on the edge of the bed, massaging his temples.

"Are you watching the news?" was all that Dallas could decipher.

"No, but I can turn the TV on now."

He clicked the remote as the news anchor announced, "Police are asking for your help in locating another missing child. They are looking for a local thirteen-year-old girl. Nova Wallace was last seen wearing jeans and a Maverick's jersey. Police ask that you call 1-800-STOP-CRIME with any information."

"Isn't that the same girl we selected to have lunch with you? The one from the foster home?" Adrian asked. "I remember her waving excessively at you during the presentation."

Dallas hit the mute button on the remote and scratched his head. "It could be her. Man, this is madness." He slapped his thigh. "She's the third young girl to go missing this week. The foundation is so important; our children are going missing at an alarming rate."

"I'll keep you posted," Hernandez said. "I hope she is found safe and not like the others. They've all had such difficult lives."

"Life can be hard on some people. Harder than it should be," Dallas said. "This proves all the more why we're on the right track."

* * *

As Alicia conditioned her hair, she recalled the day she first met Dallas in person. She wasn't entirely sure why the Charity Auction for the Paul Alexander Foundation drew her attention and made her travel from Chicago to Plano, Texas. Yet, she stood in stilettos for what seemed to be an eternity awaiting the grand prize, Dallas Avery—bachelor extraordinaire. Ladies primped and primed then sashayed closer to the podium, sure to be seen by the NBA star. As soon as a long-legged, strawberry blonde female with striking green eyes spoke into the microphone, the crowd hushed. Dallas walked out onto the stage, and the women giggled like schoolgirls, oohing and awing as though in heat.

"I don't have time for any of this nonsense." Alicia turned to make her way through the crowds towards the exit door. "Pardon me. Excuse me."

Women were packed in tighter than Ru Paul's Spanx.

"Folks," the emcee said into the mic. "Let's get this done." The applause was near deafening. Alicia was halfway to the door when she heard, "And the winner for dinner—oh, that rhymed," she said with a laugh. "Is … Alicia Mitchell from Chicago."

It took several moments to register, and her hand went in the air for a Miss America wave. "That's me," she said.

Alicia spun around to see Dallas, clad in a stunning black tuxedo walking in her direction. She watched him eying the way the strapless emerald gown perfectly accentuated each curve. Alicia may have won the auction, but he looked as if he'd won the prize.

That night set into motion events that would change both their lives.

The sound of Dallas entering the bathroom snapped her from the memories.

"Do you want to come back in with me?" Alicia asked with a husky voice.

"I don't know where you get your energy," he said. "But you may want to eat something before you attempt to go into overtime." He leaned back and bellowed a hearty laugh. "Or should I say, double overtime? Where'd you like to go to eat?"

Turning off the faucets, she stepped into the awaiting towel and reached for a second one to dry her hair. "I have an idea—let's have an outing."

Chapter 3

Something New

"I can't believe I'm going to finally use this thing." Dallas opened a door just before the entrance into the kitchen. "My mother gave this to me as a Christmas gift a few years ago." Moving a few boxes to the side, he nearly got on all fours to stretch to the far back end of the closet. "Here it is. Will this do?"

Taking the basket, Alicia read, "Newbury Basket."

"My mom said the navy blue and burgundy colors were masculine, and I suspect she hoped it would inspire me to be impulsive and think outside the box."

Turning it over a few times, Alicia opened the basket and nodded in appreciation. "It looks brand new," she said.

Dallas unbuckled the brown leather straps that held four white bone

China plates, a complete set of silverware, and heavy crystal drinking glasses. "I guess I never had to use it until now." He carried them to the sink and placed them in the steaming water.

"Your mother has excellent taste." She washed and dried the items, then returned them to the basket. Alicia turned to see Dallas checking his screen. "Is everything alright?"

His head snapped upwards as he placed the cell in his pocket. "Everything's good. Just a little misunderstanding. What do you need me to do?"

She arched an eye but said nothing. Together they chopped, sliced, and diced carrots, strawberries, apples, and celery. Dallas reached into the cabinet and pulled down a bottle of Spanish olives.

"Would you like to learn a quick recipe?" Alicia asked over her shoulder as she viewed all items in the fully stocked fridge.

Scratching his head, he pouted. "I make a mean peanut butter and jelly sandwich. Is that gourmet enough for our outing?"

Laughing, she gave him a trust me look. "Come on, don't be intimidated. Antipasto squares will be a breeze to make."

"What would you like me to do?"

"First, preheat the oven to 350 degrees," she said, selecting a package of crescent dough, turkey ham, provolone cheese, Swiss cheese, hard salami, pepperoni, and green, red, and yellow peppers from the fridge.

Eyeing the mountain of items collecting on the island, he said, "I thought you said this would be easy?"

"It'll be. When you're not making your world-famous peanut butter and jelly sandwiches, where do you enjoy dining out?" Alicia stooped down to investigate the lower cabinets.

Warm water rinsed away the lather from his hands, "I'm co-owner of Tate's with my cousin. So, I guess by default, that's the one."

"It has a Motown theme, right?"

He nodded while opening the closet door to retrieve an apron.

Locating a cutting board and knives, she asked, "What's their specialty?"

"Fried chicken, collard greens, four-cheese macaroni and cheese, sweet potatoes, and fried green tomatoes."

Dallas flickered a gaze at the fruits and vegetables. "Well, we aren't creating anything quite that extravagant, but you'll enjoy it, I promise," she said.

Alicia put her index and middle finger in the air, "Scout's honor. First, unroll the dough and place it on the bottom of the baking dish."

Dallas used a spoon to open the can of rolls, and Alicia jumped when it popped. They both laughed. "Always hate when that happens. Now what?"

"Next, you'll layer the meats, cheese, and peppers on top of the dough."

Swishing his hands up and down, "Like this?"

Examining it like a teacher overlooking mid-terms, "Perfectly done. You get a gold star." He beamed with pride at his concoction.

"Will you pull a bowl down? It's too high for me to reach."

Dallas playfully stroked her head and mouthed "Short stack" as he brought down the mixing bowl.

"After I beat the eggs lightly, you can stir in the parmesan cheese and black pepper. Then pour 3/4 of this mixture over the peppers."

He enjoyed being in the kitchen with her, so much so that he started to do a little dance.

"Before you start doing the moonwalk, MJ, we still need to unroll the second package of dough and place it over the top of the peppers. Then our final step is to brush the remaining egg mixture over it all and—"

"Then cover it," he said, pulling off a sizeable amount of aluminum foil and placing the dish in the oven. "Hernandez called to inform me about a missing teenaged girl who we selected as part of a new initiative we're doing for children in Foster Care."

She carried the bowl, mixing utensils, and baking dish, to the sink. "That is so sad. Is there any information on where she might be?"

"So far, the news is only reporting that Nova is missing." Dallas walked to the window and glanced out. "Get this, she was wearing the jersey we gave her when she learned she would be having lunch with us."

"I hope this ends well; sadly though, far too often, our children go missing and are never found."

After a few moments, he asked how long the food should remain in the oven. "Let it bake for twenty-five minutes, then cut it into squares."

Dallas placed fruit and veggies into reusable containers, packed them into the basket, selected a few bottles of fruit-flavored sparkling water, and then gathered and folded four linen napkins. Dallas pulled out a large blanket, pillows, and sunscreen as they waited for the oven's timer to sound.

* * *

"We're all set," he said as they left and settled on the front seats of the Buick Cascada. Before he hit the button to raise the garage door, he let down the top.

"Nice, we're riding topless." Alicia placed her left hand on his thigh and tapped it to the beat of Prince's Black Sweat echoing in through the radio.

"You have to love endorsement deals." His smile broadened.

The weather was perfect as they drove along President George Bush Turnpike.

Pointing out the passenger window, he said, "Way over there is the Gleneagles Country Club. As a kid, I dreamed about being a member there."

She placed a hand over his. "What was it like the day you joined?"

"It was as if I achieved a huge milestone. The inside is grander than I ever could have imagined. The views from the course take your breath away."

"I didn't know you played golf."

"I don't," he frowned. "I should say, not well. It's a spectacular location for weddings."

Dallas put a steely gaze on her. Alicia allowed the last word to linger before asking about their destination. Dallas explained that the art located within the Texas Sculpture Garden was produced by artists living in large and small cities throughout Texas.

Alicia's nod nearly became whiplash as a car that failed to signal abruptly crossed the lanes and cut them off. "I wish people would learn to drive. That's one of my main complaints about being in the city." He smacked the steering wheel and engaged the horn while slamming on his breaks. "Idiot."

She placed her left hand on his shoulder; he exhaled before she asked, "Why did you select this location?"

After a few seconds, the scowl disappeared, and he turned his head in her direction. "It's truly spectacular. Everywhere you look, you see a work of art, either manmade or made by nature. Wait and see, you'll love it. Austin is home to the most amazing restaurants as well."

"We'll have to put some of them on our list of places to try."

"After Tate's, of course," he said.

"Of course."

Several ear-piercing shrieks blared through the radio. "This is an Amber Alert for a missing fourteen-year-old African-American girl. She was last seen wearing a Mavericks jersey and cut-off jeans. She has waist-length micro-braids, brown eyes, dimples, and a chipped front tooth. The public is encouraged to contact 1-800-STOP-CRIME should you see her. We now have a message from her Foster mother."

A brief sound of rustling papers was followed by sniffs and a faint cough. "Hello, hello. My name is Dedra, and Blayze, if you can hear me, honey. We love you. We're all looking for you. Don't give up hope. We're going to find you."

"That was a message by the Foster mother of the missing child. Police are now considering it an abduction. She was last seen driving with a black male in a white convertible. Police have not yet identified the make and model."

"When James and I were younger," Alicia said. "There were times I feared for our lives. Just hearing the words, Foster care, causes my stomach to knot, and my throat tightens."

"This is insane. Hernandez called earlier today," Dallas said as he signaled before merging into the fast lane. "A few players have come together to form a nonprofit organization specializing in rescuing children entangled in human trafficking."

Commentators squawked in the background about their speculations of what happened. "Sadly," one was saying. "Our community has seen this story play out far too many times."

"Exactly," a raspy-voiced female chimed in. "Rarely does it make even the back page of the once-a-month newspaper."

"We all know why—"

There was a collective, "Umm."

"But let it happen to a young, blue-eyed pageant queen, and it's front-page international news."

Alicia's brows furrowed slightly as she shifted in her seat. "I don't like when the race card is played in every situation. Granted, it might be the case, but we don't have to play it so early in the game."

A few moments of silence expanded before she added, "Did my situation in Scotland have anything to do with this foundation?"

"I wouldn't say directly, but I'm certain indirectly. When Adrian realized the circumstances surrounding your disappearance and you recall that, he immediately set into motion a plan to rescue you."

"How could I ever forget." Alicia's eyes glazed over as her heart pounded violently in her chest. Her palms began to sweat as a tear slowly rolled down her cheek. In an instant, she was back in a vault in Scotland, fighting for her life.

Dallas turned his head in her direction when she stopped speaking. He gently touched her forearm.

Blinking back tears, she said, "I'm eternally indebted to him. I don't even want to imagine what the outcome might have been having he not acted so quickly and sent help when he did."

"Because of what happened to you," he said. "Adrian realized we could render assistance and help countless others, especially young girls. The organization will operate very much like the Underground Railroad." Dallas tapped the lever to the left of the steering wheel, and the windshield wipers swished from side to side. Fluid splashed the glass, and droplets landed on their arms. "Individuals are on standby to offer emergency shelter, food, clothing, cash, transportation in and out of countries. Police, politicians, and those in the court system are involved. Sex trafficking is a 150-billion-dollar a year industry. People are bound to be upset about the work we're doing." He shook his head. "Trafficking involves forced labor, marriage, prostitution, and also organ removal."

Opening the glovebox, she took out two napkins and wiped his arm, then hers, "The dangerous part is, there are individuals who should be helping but are part of the problem." Dallas nodded. "What measures were put in place to ensure they could trust the people in the Railroad?"

He glanced her way. "I had the same question. This is something that was already in existence. He just tapped into it and by adding our names and fame. It brought visibility and funding."

"What did they name it?"

"A Place to Ponder based on his great-grandmother's last name. On the surface, it looks like a standard mobile library and literacy center, so they can move throughout communities without raising suspicion. The true mission is to make it visible and accessible to those in need."

"That's brilliant."

They continued discussing the program as the breeze washed over them. "I'm glad you suggested an outing," he said. "It gives us a perfect opportunity to take a time-out to relax and get some fresh air."

"Perhaps we might purchase an original work of art for the condo as well," Alicia added. "Who knows? It may prove to be a wise investment."

Dallas appreciated her knowledge of basketball and the confidence with which she spoke about finances. They talked the entire afternoon into the early evening about dreams, goals, and desires. Alicia shared a few stories of her childhood, making sure not to delve too deeply into the dark, sordid details but enough for them to feel connected. Dallas shared a bit about his family and his rise to fame.

Of all the women he knew, most wanted to spend his money. Alicia, on the other hand, spoke of ways he could make money in his sleep. She spoke his love language.

Chapter 4

Maverick's Fan

Following the lunch, Dallas packed the items into the vehicle, and they walked to the park. Taking her hand into his as they strolled, he asked, "Did I tell you my first impression of you?"

Alicia's head tilted slightly as her brows arched. "Oh, do tell," she said.

"It isn't like that," he said. "Well, first, I watched you. Even before I took the stage."

Alicia stopped in her tracks; her lips parted, but no words were spoken.

"As you moved from the bidding stations to the artwork, your poise, sensuality, and strength came through immediately."

A young couple pushing a stroller walked by them. The husband's head snapped back as they passed. He immediately whispered to his wife, then did a one-eighty and headed their way. "Mr. Avery, sorry to interrupt, but do you mind if my wife and I have a photo with you? We're huge fans." His eyes glazed over as he spoke.

"Not at all," Dallas answered. "Do you have a camera?"

The wife quickly pushed the buggy slightly to the left, reached into the diaper bag then held out a cell. Alicia took it, and at the count of three, snapped a few pictures.

"My goodness, my mom is never going to believe this," she shrieked, practically rocking on her heels. "Thank you, Mr. Avery."

"Call me Dallas, and you're most welcome." Bending over and looking into the baby stroller, he asked, "What's the baby's name?"

Her face and neck turned pink, then bright red as she stammered, "Well, you're never going to believe it. But our son's name is ... Dallas."

"Really?" Dallas slid another glance at the reddish blonde hair child, "Indeed, you are fans."

She rapidly shook her head and explained, "We're huge fans, but not that huge." Her jaw dropped, then her mouth slammed shut, "I didn't mean any harm. He's named after my grandfather."

Laughing with a nudge to Alicia, he said, "No harm done. It would have been quite a mission to maintain my reputation knowing you'd named your son after me."

The couple thanked them again and continued onward to the playground.

"Do you ever grow tired of not having personal space?" she asked once out of earshot.

"It took a while, but you can't be in the business that requires fans and not like to interact with them. Most are very polite and respectful."

She contemplated this for several moments as he laced their fingers. "I guess. You were telling me about impressions."

"I tried to hold in a chuckle when you held out that glossy photo of me supplied by the foundation."

Alicia raised both hands palm out and said, "All I wanted was an autograph."

"I know. And you had your pen posed as you tapped the edge of the photo. What is it that you said?" He scratched his head.

"Oh, you're really digging it in, aren't you? I said, 'Dinner isn't necessary.'"

"I thought you were going to be stampeded right then and there. All those hungry women were eyeing me like the Last Supper, and you were the only one invited. Then you didn't want to accept the invitation." Dallas genuinely looked deflated, and she immediately regretted her initial response.

"Oh, I felt the fangs coming out immediately," she said.

They both laughed at the memory.

"In my defense, I had a plane to catch; the red-eye waits for no one. And for the record, you seemed like entirely too much work." Alicia shrugged her left shoulder, lowered her chin, and pursed her lips in his direction.

Dallas could do nothing but grin. He was sometimes too much for himself. "Touché. What I remember the most was you forming your luscious lips to announce, 'I'm not a Maverick's fan; I'm a Bull's fan.' I thought they were going to eat you for lunch."

"They would have if given the opportunity," she said.

Flashing his famous megawatt smile, he shot back, "I hope by now, you're glad you missed that flight?"

"Don't get too cocky. We're still taking this thing one day at a time."

"So, you say."

That night, they slept intertwined, and for the first time, he felt complete. Alicia was becoming the Ying to Dallas' Yang.

Chapter 5

Unexpected

Nova immediately startled and tried to open her eyes, but they were taped shut. A sense of complete darkness invaded her awareness and flowed throughout her entire body. She felt hot breath on her neck and the smell of stale cigars and cheap whiskey. Memories flooded her mind like a tsunami. She tried to fight, but her arms or legs wouldn't move. The sound of metal clanked as she struggled.

She jerked then whimpered as a sharp pricking sensation hit her left arm. Her head went limp and flopped to the side. She recalled something her grandmother had once told her. You are stronger than you'll ever know, Nova. Keep fighting, and even death must bow down. Even if her body couldn't move, she was determined to stay alive.

"Next delivery," the man said in a thick German accent. "Make sure to call me first. She smells. I like fresh merchandise."

"My apologies, my friend. Let me make it up to you." Nova's torso shuddered as a slight breeze brushed over her abdomen then down through her pelvis.

Tiny bumps and beads of sweat emerged over every inch of her body, and she shivered. Nova recognized the second voice as the man who'd given her tickets to the banquet. Her body shook uncontrollably. This was no dream; it was a nightmare.

"See, we always take care of our clients," he said as he opened the door behind him. "This is Blayze. She is our newest inventory."

Strong hands gripped Nova's throat and remained until darkness deeper than fear invaded her entire soul. Grandma.

* * *

Alicia woke to the request of Dallas asking for her to spend one more day. As with the previous days, she agreed. He was already dressed and, on the phone, when she entered the kitchen.

"Morning," he said, ending the call.

She gave him a quick kiss on the lips. "Hello to you. You're up early. Is everything okay?"

He glanced at the phone in his hand. "You mean this? Everything is excellent. Better than perfect. That was Katie, and I was giving her some updated information."

Alicia walked over to the stove and poured hot water into the French press. At the same time, Dallas retrieved a container of Half-n-Half from the refrigerator.

"Thank you." She side-stepped his love tap on her rear end, prepared the coffee, and took a seat next to him. "I enjoyed yesterday. That was very refreshing. I needed to be reset."

"You and me both," he said as he leaned in and kissed her forehead.

"What would you like to do today? Any plans?"

Hesitating, she traced the edges of her cup with her fingertip.

"Is there something you need to tell me?" A wry expression passed over his face. He reached for a glass of water and took a sip.

"Dallas, this has been wonderful. I mean, it truly has. And as I told you, I would've been content with simply having your autograph—"

"What're you saying, Alicia?"

She stood and took a few steps away. "Dallas, playing house isn't my style. I've been here far longer than either of us intended. We have to put an end to this eventually."

"Why? I don't understand. What can I do to change your mind?" With just one step, he lessened the space between them. "What if we use this time to work?"

Alicia's brows furrowed, and she leaned slightly away from him. "What do you mean by 'work'?"

"Not that! I mean, strategize." He walked to the window just as a neighbor exited the building, walking a grey and white miniature Shiatzu. "You're good with accounting, investments, and moving money around, right?"

"I am. So?" She cocked her head back as if expecting him to deliver a punchline to a poorly executed joke.

"What if…" He placed two hands on her shoulders and looked deeply into her eyes. "While you're here, you give me pointers about money matters. I haven't been receiving the returns on my investments like I anticipated. I could use some assistance, and I trust you." When her response was slow to come, he stepped back to the window just as the Shiatzu squatted on the lawn. "We only briefly touched on the topic your first hours here. Why not use this as an opportunity to delve deeper," he reasoned.

"Ahem." Her head snapped in his direction. "By 'deeper,' you mean money matters, correct?"

"Of course." He placed his first two fingers up. "Scout's honor."

Alicia paused a few minutes before responding. She wanted to put some distance between them to cool the flame threatening to burn out of control. Her level of comfort with Dallas was frightening. However, she wouldn't want to miss the opportunity to share her knowledge of increasing his rates of returns, either. "Okay, then. I'll agree to a few more days, but soon, I will need to go home."

He pumped his fists into the air as though he'd won an NBA Championship. "Deal. We can begin right away."

She frowned at the fact he didn't address the part of the statement that meant she would leave.

Their lovemaking didn't require nakedness, bubble bath, or being thrust up against a wall to be fulfilling. That afternoon, they discussed ways to ensure Dallas' money worked for him years after he could no longer hold a basketball or discuss the game. "I want to tell you how your money can multiply while you're sleeping," she said. Dallas experienced a deep, warming, tingling sensation throughout his entire being.

Mid-afternoon, they paused long enough to prepare dinner. Dallas wasn't a good cook, but he was a great assistant. Alicia made spinach, turkey bacon alfredo with angel hair pasta, and a broccoli salad.

"Dallas, do you mind mixing a few drinks as we wait for the pasta to finish?"

Wiping his hands on a paper towel, he asked, "What would you like?"

"Surprise me."

Taking a sip, she voiced approval. "Oh, this is delicious. What is it?"

Bowing theatrically, he answered. "I'm glad you like my mixology skills. It's called a Moscow mule."

"It's perfect." Alicia scooped two healthy portions of pasta and salad for him and a much smaller amount for herself. She bowed her head, awaiting his prayer.

"Lord, I thank you for this meal and for the hands that prepared it. May it be nourishment to our bodies to empower us to do your will."

Together they said, "Amen."

Dallas shoveled the food into his mouth as if it were luggage forced into the x-ray machine at an airport security gate.

"Where do you put all of that food?" she inquired.

"I, like most athletes, have a great metabolic system. Besides, I normally don't enjoy home cooking like this unless I'm visiting my mom. I have to get it in when I can."

"Geez. Could you slow down just a bit? I'm scared to put my hand on the table for fear it will be shoved into your mouth, too."

"Now, that's an idea."

"Dallas, listen to me," she admonished. "Take time to savor your meal the same way you do with me."

He winked as he reached for the serving utensil and heaped another portion onto his now empty plate. Dallas complied, and she felt a sliver of relief.

"Tell me more about ways I may diversify my portfolio," he asked while wiping the corner of his mouth with a linen napkin.

She stood, collecting their plates, rinsed them, and placed them in the dishwasher. At the same time, Dallas transferred the leftovers to a reusable container and put them in the fridge. "Let's go into the living room to talk about it," she said as he started the dishwasher.

"Woman, you're talking my language." He sat and looked deeply into her eyes. "I'm thankful your name was called as the winner and even more thankful it rained."

"You mean you're glad I got doused in that downpour?"

"That too. Without it, you would never have come to my house." He pulled his wallet out of his back pocket. "I need to get the name and address of that cloud and send it a nice fat check."

"Do you really think Mother Nature lets her clouds accept payments from an American Express?"

"She might if I use a Centurion Card?" he countered.

They both laughed as they continued chatting and drinking. Dallas could feel his bottom line swelling as much as his desire for Alicia.

* * *

Sobs resonated from the back room of the dimly lit house. "I want to go home."

"Shhhh, don't cry, or he'll come back." A small voice warned. "You won't like it if you make him mad."

Footsteps sounded down the hall coming in their direction. "Hurry, pretend you're asleep."

Their breathing silenced as the steps grew nearer. The knob creaked, and the door slowly opened. Bright light flooded into the small space. Large, red-streaked eyes quickly squeezed shut. A little girl with afro puff ponytails slapped a hand across the mouth of the girl cowering on the bed beside her. Terror filled her expression as large hands hard as steel snatched her by the hair and completely lifted her off the mattress.

The room erupted with screams, "No! Don't take her! Stop."

"Shut up." The loud click of the revolver created a deafening silence in the room. "No need to make yourselves known. You'll all get a turn." He laughed so forcefully, he coughed then gagged. "Be patient." He stormed out, dragging the screaming child behind him.

"Why are they doing this to us?" a girl with freckles and reddish-brown hair cried from under the covers, too flimsy to protect them from the frigid chill. "What did we do?" Her cries muffled in the dingy thin pillow. "I wish I never entered that contest."

"Me too," came a faint cry.

"Me too," came an echo from others.

Chapter 6

Nickel & Nickel

"Dallas, could you please assist me?" Alicia admired her reflection in the full-length mirror. Even though she was nearly twice Dallas' age, not many seemed to notice, especially him.

"Wow! You look spectacular." He eyed her from the top of her head to her pink-painted toes. A slow whistle escaped his pursed lips. "I'm going to be the envy of a lot of fellas tonight." He held his palm up to receive hers. Once she touched his fingers, Dallas twirled Alicia around in circles.

"Baby, stop before I get dizzy." Smoothing down the dress from her waist to just above her knee, she asked, "You like it?"

"I don't just like it. I love it." Dallas gripped the zipper just above the edge of the lace thong and slowly pulled it up. He kissed alongside her spine as he did.

Speaking to the reflection in the mirror, she scolded, "Your tongue's going to get stuck in that zipper if you aren't careful."

Raising his head to scan the image of the two of them staring back at him. He countered, "Oh, I have skills with this tongue that ensures it's never stuck anywhere it doesn't want to be."

Alicia turned to face him. "You look very debonaire yourself." She kissed him on the left cheek while adjusting his tie. "One last bit of assistance before you walk out." She handed him a triple strand of pearls and turned her back.

Dallas's hands went limp by his side. "Are you sure you're comfortable wearing pearls?" his voice just above a whisper.

Without skipping a beat, she replied, "I survived so much in Scotland. At one point, I didn't think we'd make it out of there alive. Even after all that occurred, I refuse to let myself become a victim. To change what I wear, where I go, or do, would be defeat. He'd win."

Dallas brought the necklace over her head then up to her neck. After a few attempts, he connected the clasps and gave it a gentle tug ensuring it was locked. "Perfect," he announced.

Giving a little curtsy, she said, "I'll be down in a few moments. I just need to put on a pair of heels and touch up my makeup."

"With a face nearly perfect, I'd better hurry. You won't spend but a second if that."

In under five minutes, stilettoes clicked down the stairs. He opened the front door. "After you, madam."

* * *

"Where're we going?" Alicia glanced out the passenger window as he turned left on North Avenue.

Signaling his intent to change lanes, he said, "I thought I'd treat you to the finest Italian restaurant in Plano—"

Sitting up and clasping her hands together, "Are we going to Antonio V's?"

Flashing a toothy grin, he confirmed. "We are indeed."

"Excellent choice."

They discussed their love of Italian foods and wines as Luther Vandross crooned A House is Not a Home. The Buick Enclave resembled a talent show audition more than a vehicle. They were still singing as he drove to the front entrance on West North Avenue.

"You know, with our love of food, we should start a cooking show," he said as he parked the vehicle.

"Now you're talking my language." Alicia tapped her cheek as if formulating a workable plan. "We could call it F-Squared."

His eyebrow winged, "You mean food and—"

"Finances. Food and finances." She added quickly.

"That works too," he teased as he turned off the ignition. "Can the show have three words?"

"Ma'am…" The valet excitedly opened the door before she might respond.

"Thank you." Alicia's long legs exited the car eliciting stares from passersby.

Dallas loved the looks he received with Alicia on his arm. He felt like a king with his queen and grew several inches taller with each step. "The way you are killin' it in that dress, we may name it Murder, Mystery, and Mayhem.

* * *

Dallas passed the keys to a long-legged valet with a sun-kissed tan. Her brows winged as her head cocked slightly to the left.

"Welcome back, Sir."

Alicia shot Dallas a look. "Were you here recently?"

Shaking his head, he replied, "No, not for a year or so."

Sarvanti's face flushed red. Be the fly on the wall. Her mouth opened wide, then clamped shut. She quickly slid behind the driver's seat and immediately parked the car.

Several valets glanced awkwardly towards Dallas and then to their phones. Alicia gave him a quizzical glance but continued walking alongside him.

Massive, framed images of Dante Alighieri, Marco Polo, Sophia Loren, and Marco Balotelli greeted them. They were escorted to a table by a young, clean-cut waiter who reminded Alicia of Bruno Mars.

"I'll be a few moments. I want to stop in the men's room."

"Are you feeling well?" she inquired. "Do we need to leave?"

Waving off her concern. "Everything is fine. I'll be right out."

The host led Alicia to the table. After she was seated, he said, "Rafiki will be your server. Enjoy your meal."

* * *

"Adrian, I got your text. What's going on?"

"Something strange is happening. I got a call from the credit card company because of some unusual charges. A few of the members of the organization have experienced the same occurrence. It also appears that someone has been sending out invitations to young girls in the Foster care agency with the organization's information."

"It seems we have upset a few powers that be." Dallas scratched his forehead. "Watch your back, brother."

"I will, and you do the same. I'll keep you posted."

Moments later, Rafiki Bakari stood near their table. His six-foot frame nearly eclipsed the illumination from the decorative sconces on the walls. Alicia looked up to see a set of amber eyes framed by flawless bronze skin. She quickly turned in the opposite direction and exhaled.

"Ma'am, welcome to Antonio V's Ristorante." He pronounced each word with a perfect Italian accent. His gaze lingered, and Alicia shifted in her seat. "Have you dined with us before?"

"I haven't but—"

"Mr. Avery?" Rafiki turned his entire body away from her and towards Dallas as he approached the table.

"I apologize, Mr. Avery," he said, quickly glancing over his massive shoulders to see if management caught wind of his groupie moment. "I'll be right back."

"You relish in the fanfare, don't you?" Alicia asked once they were alone. "Never mind, your grin answered my question."

"I think this belongs to you, Sir?" Rafiki passed Dallas a credit card. "We were just about to mail it back to the company when we couldn't find a phone number for you."

The older gentleman at an adjacent table dropped his drink. Glass, ice, and liquid spilled all over the floor. "I'll be right back," Rafiki announced.

Dallas reached into his front jacket pocket, removed his wallet, and then counted his cards. "This is absurd." He compared it to his card, and his brow furrowed. "All the numbers are the same, but this is not my signature."

"What are you going to do with it?" Alicia looked over his arm, examining the card with him.

Placing the card in an empty slot, he said, "I'm going to hold on to it. It's a clone."

The waiter returned, apologizing.

"Hey, no need at all." Dallas returned his wallet to the pocket. "Let's do this." Dallas reached for the tablet in the man's hand. "What if I autograph this for you, and we'll keep it between the two of us."

Nodding but saying, "Oh no. You don't need to do that." His smile said contrary.

"No problem at all." Dallas signed the paper and tilted the pen to Alicia.

Waving and grinning, "I'm certain mine will add little to no value, thank you."

Rafiki again blinked and shook himself. "Would you like to begin with a drink?" He directed to Dallas.

"We'll have a bottle of Nickel & Nickel."

"Excellent choice." Rafiki nodded his approval. "I'll place your drink order and return with bread."

Dallas placed his hand over hers. His eyes lingered on hers. "I'm so excited to share this experience with you. Thank you for hanging with me."

Batting her eyes, she teased, "Oh, does this mean you want my autograph, kind sir?" She reached into her purse to grab a pen.

"How about we table that until after dessert? Maybe take care of that following breakfast," he said with a husky voice.

Tucking her chin into her left shoulder, her eyes widened. "What sort of lady do you take me for? I don't kiss on first dates." This comment caused Dallas to laugh so loudly the elderly man seated next to them looked up from his plate of Capellini Siciliana. Eggplant, red peppers, and capers dangled at the edge of his suspended fork. His brain awaited following through on the motion he had been doing nonstop for the previous seven minutes. Alicia first noticed him when he failed to look up from his plate. That must be some darn good pasta, she thought as they were seated.

Dallas gave him the carry-on, nothing to see here glance. Recognition registered in the man's gaze, but his fork captured his attention more than being a fan did. He chomped down on his fork, causing the handle to jerk in his right hand.

Alicia shook her head.

Chapter 7

Black and Gold Marble

Tilting her head back and giving him a slightly more serious posture. "Tell me about your childhood. What was it like growing up Dallas?"

He pulled his hand back from hers and placed them in his lap. After a few moments of silence, Alicia opened her mouth to repeat the question, but Rafiki returned with the wine.

Pouring a small amount in one glass and passing it to Dallas, he awaited the signal to continue. Dallas sipped and nodded as the glass was partially filled, followed by the second.

"To us," he lifted his cut-crystal glass to hers.

Clinking the glass against the one in his hand, "Indeed."

They made their entrée selections as Rafiki retrieved the menus. A young girl with striking blue eyes, dimples, and a buzz-cut brought fresh baked bread and butter on a wooden platter.

Once alone, Alicia whispered, "I believe you could have ordered corn dogs and tater tots and he would have said, 'Excellent choice.'"

Dallas agreed. After taking a generous sip of wine. "My childhood was more chaotic than the life I have planned out for myself." He closed his eyes for a few moments before speaking again. Raising his lids, he locked eyes with a little boy around the age of four. Dallas realizedhe had been staring from his booster seat.

"It's gonna be okay, okay, mister," he said as blonde curls bounced up and down as his dimpled cheeks puff with air.

Looking astonished, the father quickly redirected the child. "Spencer, remember, I taught you not to interrupt people while they're eating." Suddenly turning to Dallas, "We're teaching him Mindfulness and how to speak to his emotions. He must have mistaken your eyes being closed as something being the matter. Wait. Aren't you—"

Forcing a smile, "I am." To the lad, he said, "Thank you for your kind words, Spencer. That was very perceptive of you." Dallas reaches into his breast pocket to retrieve a white envelope. "These were for a friend who is unable to attend due to a family emergency. Please accept this as my gift to little Spence here for his kindness."

The father hesitated, but the wife removed the envelop and opened it immediately. "Thank you, Mr. Avery. We'll put these to excellent use." She tucked the gift deep within her purse. "We'll allow our friends to eat their dinner in peace, right?" The son mimicked the mom's nod, then did an about-face and focused on his macaroni n' cheese.

Alicia mouthed, "I need to use the lady's room." Leaning over to kiss him on the cheek, "That was very kind of you."

Dallas beamed. As she walked away, he felt his heart violently beating within the walls of his chest. He wouldn't have believed it had the world-famous psychic Edgar Cayce glanced into a crystal ball and told him he would one day fall head over balls in love with a woman nearly twice his age.

Hell, Dallas hadn't simply fallen in love. The thought of losing her again nearly arrested his very breath. When only together for ten short days, Alicia left for Scotland. Dallas vividly recalled the feeling of his heart practically fractured into a million tiny pieces, each bearing her name. Since that day, Dallas feared she might second guess any romantic gestures. Her late husband, Patrick's guise, to marry her because of her direct connection with a hidden fortune was a blow to her frail memories of their relationship.

Patrick. May you rot in hell. Dallas had never met the man, but he hated him for what he'd done to Alicia. If he weren't already dead, Dallas believed in the center of his being, he'd catch a case for Alicia. He loved her that much.

* * *

The ladies' restroom was luxury overload. Faucets that resembled solid blocks of gold extended from the floor to near waist-high height flanked the back wall. Sconces in the same liquid gold texture hung perfectly alongside mirrors that resembled pieces of artwork rather than items upon which to check reflections.

The wall was not to be outdone by the faucets. They were floor-to-ceiling single pieces of black marble with deep gold marbling throughout. The reflection of the lights caused miniature fairies to flit and twirl as Alicia made her way to the stall.

There was no expense spared in here, she thought as she gently placed the disposable cover over the elongated porcelain toilet seat. As Alicia admired the door honed from a single ancient tree, multiple footsteps entered the room. Desperately attempting to recall if there were more stalls, she stopped noticing the décor and froze.

"Megan, did you see Dallas Avery out there?" The sound of the woman's voice was placed around the age of twenty-two, max. Alicia cracked the door slightly. The accent was slightly mid-western with a slight lisp. Her ivory complexion and platinum blond hair revealed hours of conditioning and care. The blonde reached into a Louis Vuitton to retrieve lipstick.

Leaning in for a closer look, Megan said, "I really like that color, Quin. Which one is it?"

Turning over the tube, she read, "Chanel Le Vernis Coup de Coeur 609," then slathered on a generous amount. She smacked her lips together then made a popping sound. "It's one of my favorites."

Megan retrieved it from extended manicured fingertips, applied a thin layer, then returned it. Contrary to her friend's monotone physical appearance, her olive skin was a stark contrast to her ebony tresses. The plum lip color brought her features together beautifully. "To answer your question, of course, I saw him."

"He's such a beautiful specimen of a man. I'd love to see him palm this," Quin said, then turned her backside towards the mirror and patted her ass. "You think he could handle all this action?" Her toned buttocks bulged tightly against the leather mini skirt, causing the stitches to gap as she rolled her hips in a figure-eight motion.

"How did you pour yourself into that thing?" Megan asked. The black off-the-shoulder dress revealed beautiful genes or dedicated hours in the gym, or a combination of both. She twisted from side to side, admiring her reflection in the mirror.

Megan continued talking. "Isn't that the same woman who won the auction seated with him?"

Quin checked her makeup and Alicia noticed she had heterochromia iridium. One iris was crystal blue the other light brown with specs of copper and green. Pleased with her reflection, she turned on the water, then pressing the lever until a generous amount of soap formed in her palm, "You must think I'm a walking memory stick. How would I remember? That event was eighty days ago. And if you don't recall, we were three sheets to the wind that night," Quin said.

Laughing, Megan agreed. "How old do you think she is? I mean, she looks good no matter how old, great even—

"Can you see him being serious with someone her age?" Quin jibed. "I read in one of his interviews he wants kids and all that jazz."

While drying her hands with one of the plush paper towels, Megan said, "These things are as thick and thirsty as you are." She jokingly swatted her friend's hip before tossing it in the exotically shaped gold trash container. "Besides, you have a husband, and last you said, you'd never blow your figure for kids." She placed her hands upon ample hips. "And besides, you aren't even a Maverick's fan."

Clasping her purse under her left arm, "I don't plan to actually make a kid with him, just practice really hard." Quin tilted her head towards her friend. "And, I may not be a fan of his team, but I'm definitely a fangirl of his body." She paused then added, "I still say a man of his caliber and stamina would be of better use between the sheets of someone like, let's just say…" she slung those blonde tresses over her tattooed shoulder. "Me."

Chapter 8

Reset

Alicia stood before the mirror a few additional moments after she dried her hands. Why didn't you say anything? She chastised her reflection in the full-length mirror. She didn't need a response. The reason had nothing to do with being too much of a lady. Alicia was as much street as she was a saint. The real reason was that the words echoed her inner thoughts. A chance encounter in a public bathroom exposed all her inner fears. She had come face to face with them.

Inner fears should never become outer realities. Leaving, Alicia held her head high as she swung her full hips from side to side. Each step oozed sensuality. As she sashayed, heads turned from men and women to include the men accompanying the bathroom buddies. As the ladies' gaze followed the direction of their gawking husband's stares, they connected with Alicia's. She simply winked, "Hello, ladies and gentlemen."

Alicia stopped at the bar, spoke with the bartender, and returned to their table.

His brow furrowed slightly, and the napkin was neatly folded on the charger plate and not opened on his lap. "There you are. I thought I was going to have to send in a search squad. Is everything okay?" His eyes never broke contact with hers.

Waving off his concern, she replied, "As always, there was a line." Her answer seemed to quiet any further alarm because Dallas smiled and changed the subject. It might have been the arrival of the food as well that elevated his mood. Either way, Alicia let out a slight sigh of relief. Dallas didn't notice, but eagle-eyed Spencer did. Thankfully, his mother intercepted before miniature Sherlock Holmes divulged any more emotional clues.

"Thank you," said the men seated with the bathroom gossips as they held up their glasses.

"You're most welcome. I didn't want the ladies to be so thirsty..."

Both women shot her a look then quickly forced a smile.

"What was that for?" Dallas tilted his head as he spoke.

"Nothing much. Just being hospitable."

"Goodbye, Mister."

"Have a good day, little man." He put up his palm for a high-five. Spencer giggled as he jumped several times, struggling to reach Dallas' hand. After a few failed attempts, Dallas lowered it to his height. Smack.

"Thank you, Mr. Avery, for everything," the father said. "Enjoy the rest of your evening." The family left the restaurant, their son practically skipping in the middle.

"Have you ever wanted kids?" The question caught Alicia off guard and ushered in the earlier comments she'd been so successful in squelching.

Can you see him being serious with someone her age? The words echoed throughout the hidden chambers of her soul and screamed at the empty mental crib in her heart.

Chapter 9

Squad Car

Alicia's eyes opened. She listened for a moment believing perhaps she'd heard something that caused her to stir. Nothing. The only sound was Dallas snoring softly, his arm draped tightly around her as if he thought she'd flee in the night.

Have you ever thought about kids?

His question hadn't stopped reverberating in her mind.

Alicia's reaction to the question had more to do with her insecurities and suddenness of him asking than it did with the incident in the bathroom. They had seen dozens of children while out on dates. What had made last night different? Alicia loved children. But were you to ask her about having them, her response would be, "It's—complicated."

* * *

The sirens were faint in the distance, but the sound became louder the closer the squad car got to the house. She was only eight and should have been terrified, but something within her tiny soul refused to give way to fear. Alicia wasn't the one who'd committed a crime. The screams, putrid stench of fear and urine combined with the blood dripping from the edge of the blade in her hand testified otherwise.

This was her second, third, or was it the fifth foster family? She and her brother James had long stopped counting. However, this home would forever stick in her memory. For in it, she nearly lost her innocence but gained her strength.

The police took one look at the perverted degenerate and one look at her. Young, scared—she turned on the waterworks just as they walked in. Had it not been for the crooked nappy ponytails, one might have thought her to be a boy. Nothing of her body would make a trifflin' ass man believe he could treat it like a woman. Thank goodness James had given her the cutter for protection, yet even he was surprised she'd used it. And used it well.

"He won't be using that for a very long time if ever," the stocky blue-eyed officer said. His belly reminded Alicia of Santa Claus, only his teeth were stained yellow, and he smelled of stale coffee and tobacco. James nudged her because she squinted when he tried to speak. She realized she must've looked like she was seeing and smelling something disgusting.

"Do the children have any family members to stay with?" The female officer was very concerned. Her brown eyes softened against her ebony skin. Alicia guessed that she had to use all the bobby pins on the card to keep her bun so tight.

The social worker, who arrived late, used a painted finger to shuffle through a mountain of papers. Several fell to the floor. She grunted when she bent over to retrieve them. "May I sit down?" she asked the male officer.

He nodded as wide hips settled on the delipidated sofa. "I see here," she said, attempting to catch her breath. "There's a grandmother, Ms. Shahidell, we could contact." She looked up, not a single emotion displayed in her expression.

Exhaling and biting down to hold back anger, "Do you have the number? Or might that take up too much energy?" The female officer walked over to Alicia and placed a hand on her shoulder.

Taking a battered cell phone from her peeling imitation leather satchel, she punched in the digits. After a few rings, "Hello, this is Elizabeth Jurgenson, the social worker for your grandchildren, Alicia and James. A situation has come about that requires the children to be moved from their current location. May we set up a time to meet in person?" The question was followed by a few moments of silence then, "Um-hum. Okay. Right. Very well. I'll meet you then."

Just like that. The siblings were placed precisely where they wanted to be all along, with their grandmother. When she arrived, Alicia received a musical jewelry box. Each night she turned the metal key and allowed the notes to lull her to sleep.

Alicia rolled over onto her left side, away from Dallas. Reliving her painful past brought a sense of sadness resulting in tears. "What're you doing?" she whispered to herself and knew exactly what she needed to do. As he rested peacefully, she eased out of bed and tiptoed towards the door.

* * *

"I see someone is up early." Dallas stretched his long arms into the air. "Where are you off to?"

Busted. "I was going to just get some juice. Would you like a glass?" Chicken.

He patted the space in the bed she had previously occupied. "Come here first," he commanded as he raised the duvet, revealing himself to her. "Then we'll both have an appetite that'll require more than just nectar from squeezed fruit."

One glimpse had her legs moving on their own accord towards the bed and not the door.

You're so easy. Alicia's inner voice screamed.

Alicia nearly skipped back to bed. She could follow through with her plans in a little while. Make that in an hour or so.

Chapter 10

Change of Plans

Two hours later, they were showered, dressed, and sitting around the dining room table. Dallas said, "I have to go into the office for about an hour or so. It won't take me long. Katie has something for me to pick up. Would you like to ride with me?"

"I'll take care of a few things around here. Maybe toss a load of laundry in the washer."

He looked at her sideways as if not believing the response but said nothing beyond, "Okay." Since leaving the restaurant, she hadn't been responding the same. He knew his surprise would perk her up.

As soon as the door closed, Alicia leaped from her seat, rushing from room to room. She quickly made her way through the condo to gather her belongings and had them packed when—

"Where're you going?"

His voice stopped Alicia in her tracks. She was so busy grabbing things; she didn't hear the alarm chime. "I … Dallas." Silence took temporary residency in her mouth. "What're you doing back so soon?" she finally said. "The real question is, what're we doing?"

Arms crossed over his massive chest, "What do you mean?" he asked. "Why must we label everything?" Dallas sat on the nearest solid surface, which happened to be the coffee table. "To answer your question, right now, we're in my condo discussing why your bags are packed and why you waited until I left to do so?" Sadness filled his brown eyes, and it took everything within not to run to him.

Alicia lowered herself into an adjacent chair then exhaled deeply. "I've been here for," her fingers moved, and she mouthed silently. "Eighty-four days."

"Okay. And?"

"And …" standing, she spread her arms out and gestured to include their immediate area. "This was to be a one-time dinner date and an autograph, not endless weeks of us playing house."

Dallas repositioned himself in the chair beside her. He placed a hand on her shoulder, "I get it. Neither of us came into this relationship with a script. I was caught off guard as much as you were. You have to admit, though," he flashed his megawatt smile. "Our trip to Jamaica was thrilling, yes?

Nodding, "It was."

Scooting closer, he added, "And Canada was delightful, wouldn't you agree?"

A slight smile graced her lips, "It was indeed."

Tilting his head towards her, batting his eyes, "Seattle and Nashville were exciting as well, correct?"

Her posture shifted towards him as she nodded. "Dallas was my favorite place, and for obvious reasons, let's not discuss Scotland, all right?"

"I fully understand your reasonings for Scotland." He allowed a few pregnant moments to pass. "Baby, rather than focusing on what we're doing," she held up her hand to interrupt, but he kept speaking. "Let's focus on where we're doing it, shall we?"

Alicia opened her mouth to speak, but the words were slow to come. "As much as the reasoning side of my brain is telling me to pump the breaks and head for the nearest exit—" Dallas stood in protest. Alicia raised her hands, palms facing him, "But I must admit, I'm enjoying myself. Nevertheless, it's not enough, Dallas. You're going to want so much more."

Grinning from ear to ear like a Cheshire cat as he turned his attention towards the front door. "Since your bags are packed, I guess I can share my news." He pulled out a white envelope and passed it over.

Turning the envelope over a few times for a closer inspection, she sank herself in a chair, then slowly ripped off a thin section revealing the items inside. She tilted the package until the contents dropped on her lap. Tears streamed down her face, leaving a trail where her makeup once was. She moved her lips, but not a single word came out.

Easing her to the right, just enough to make room to join her in the chair. Alicia's vulnerability at that moment caused his heart to race. "Based on your reaction, I take it, you approve?"

"You didn't? I mean, you did. I mean, hell, I don't know what I mean."

Dallas scooped her into his arms and embraced her. "From the moment you told me about that musical box," he said. "I've been anxiously awaiting Katie's plan for our trip to Schloss Neuschwanstein. Or as you would say, 'Neuschwanstein Castle.' She was more excited than me. She met me at the end of the street. That's how I made it back so quickly." He looked her in the eyes. "Since you got a head start by packing, all that's needed is for me to grab a few items, my passport, and off we can go."

The waterworks started, and she couldn't cut them off. "This is the most beautiful gift anyone could have given to me."

Dallas provided a beautiful, safe place for her to fall, and Alicia was plummeting heart first.

* * *

The passengers in line simply nodded as Dallas and Alicia boarded, heading to first class. They talked the entire way to Chicago.

"Since we have two hours before we board the next flight, let's say we go for a quick drink?" Dallas asked as they walked to the next gate.

Clacking her tongue against the roof of her mouth, "I am a bit parched."

Alicia downloaded information on the castle, "Neuschwanstein Castle is a powerful symbol the world over thanks to its idealized romantic architecture," she recited. "That combined with the tragic love story of its owner, King Ludwig II of Bavaria."

"I cannot imagine all the work that went into building such a magnificent structure." He took a sip of an amber concoction. "Without modern technology, it must've taken decades to complete."

"I just read that," Alicia swiped right a few times on the cell then answered, "they began building Neuschwanstein Castle in 1869." She used a manicured finger to move the images from side to side. "It also says, 'Ludwig II brought together elements from Wartburg Castle and from the fictional Castle of the Holy Grail from Wagner's opera Parsifal.'"

Dallas scratched his forehead, "I've never heard of him. What kind of king was he?"

"That's a great question." She sipped her drink. "He actually had no real power, which is why he devoted more of his time to the fine arts." She scans through a few images in silence, then added, "He created his own fantasy world of myths and fairytales, which we can see in the Singers' Hall." Placing his knife between the tine of his right-side-up fork as it lay along the rim of the plate. He said, "You asked me a question a few days ago about my childhood."

Alicia looked up from her phone. "I recall."

"I haven't told very many people about the early chapters of my life." He lowered his voice to an intimate level but not to a sneaky hushed tone that instantly caused everyone in the room to stop talking, press in, and listen. Dallas had mastered the art of effective and elusive communication.

Alicia leaned closer. "I didn't mean for you to spill the beans on your family's sordid past. It was an attempt to get to know Dallas, the man, and not only your stats and net worth."

Dallas voiced agreeance. "It was a very appropriate question; I've never been asked it before." His eyes glazed over and appeared very distant. His physical body was still as close, but his mind, his memory, was back in time. He reminded her of an episode of The Twilight Zone she'd seen as a child.

Alicia took a sip of water.

Dallas raised a palm to his mouth as he coughed, "What I think I learned the most," he said, then took a drink from his glass. "Is the value of peace and tranquility."

Alicia deeply exhaled, "Amen to that."

"I knew without a shadow of a doubt," he continued, "that my mother loved me—and still does. But she and my pops." He shook his head as if removing a horrible memory. "They went at it all the time."

"I'm so sorry."

He didn't absorb her words. "Their battles were vicious."

"Did things become physical?"

Dallas stretched his legs, "There are scars far worse than a black eye," he said. "Pops never hit my mom, that I know of, but his verbal attacks landed harder than Muhammad Ali ever could hit on a good day." He opened then refolded the paper napkin. Clearly, a nervous action because the conversation was so sensitive. "Watching their interaction schooled me on the importance of being with someone I considered a friend as much as a mate. I learned the meaning of being unequally yoked. No matter what we did for him, that dude was never satisfied. I keep asking myself, 'What does it take to please him?' Soon I stopped trying altogether and started living my life."

She, too, learned a valuable skillset from her family. And as much as she appreciated Dallas' openness, she had no intentions today or otherwise in sharing her family's dirt. That was the plan anyway. She had no plans of opening her legs either, but that goal went flying out the window faster than her lace panties flew off. "Parents don't understand how their actions leave permanent stains on their children's souls."

His head jerked up immediately, and his brow wrinkled. "I thought I was the only person who used that phrase," he said with a low voice.

Alicia held his hand as they shared sacred space that allowed transparency and healing to flow from one soul to another. Her chest slowly rose, then fell, and her shoulders lowered from their previous resting place just beneath her ears. Her brows softened, and her chin tilted forward.

* * *

Dallas couldn't explain the perfectly terrifying attraction he had to Alicia. As he allowed the thoughts to flow through his mind, he envisioned Duke Kahanamoku masterfully riding a thirty-five-foot wave off the shores of Hawaii. Dallas was hanging ten, alright. What he feared was a complete wipe-out. Something about their chemistry and her passion made him feel like he was losing his damn mind.

Someone dropped their cutlery, and they both looked up. An older Black man with a scruffy beard bent over to retrieve the fork just as the waiter brought a new napkin-wrapped set of utensils.

Their cell phones vibrated as the announcement boomed, "Attention passengers of United Flight 3463 to Munich, Germany. There has been a change in the departure terminal. You'll now board from Gate C18."

Dallas waved for their check, and they started their way towards the updated gate.

"Whatever came of the credit card situation?" Alicia asked.

"The bank says whoever created the card did a bang-up job. Had it not been returned; I never would've known the money was going out of my account."

"What reason would someone have to clone your card? What sort of charges were on there?" Her head tilted. "Did they buy a yacht or a mansion?"

"That's the insane part. The charges were so low, it wouldn't have raised a red flag. They were mostly to restaurants and usually for two people. The bank said they're investigating it. I told them I'm traveling and not to do anything with the accounts until we return."

"Maybe someone is impersonating you?" Alicia said. "I heard about people who pretend to be celebrities to get into events, run up charges, and things like that."

"Whatever it is," he said. "It's scary to think someone is out there saying they're me."

Dallas turned his head and winked at her. "Am I moving too quickly for you?" he asked.

"Oh, don't think you can outrun me," she said, gasping for air. "I move like a gazelle when I am excited about something." And she bolted in front of him as he double-stepped to keep up.

They maneuvered past a young mother with a screaming toddler and through a gaggling dance troop excited about their first plane ride and arrived at the gate with time to spare. Dallas pointed to an empty row of seats near the window; he sat as she stared out at the vehicles carrying luggage.

"It's so amazing to me how planes remain in the air," she commented. "So many people in a huge metal apparatus soaring through the clouds defying gravity."

"Whoa," he said. "Don't get on a soapbox. He patted the empty space next to his. "Maybe while we are in Germany, I'll purchase a private jet, then it'll only be the pilot, attendant, and the two of us onboard the gravity-defying vehicle."

She dismissed his jester with a flick of her wrist as she settled in the chair beside him. "You never told me which of all the places we've visited so far was your favorite."

Dallas' disposition shifted; his features softened. "If you would've asked me last week, I would have said Paris." He placed a hand on her lap. "However, after having witnessed your reaction to us visiting Germany, hands down. Today's visit will be my favorite destination— that is unless I'm able to squeeze in one more adventure."

She gave him a 'don't push your luck, Mr.' look just as the attendant queued the mic.

The Latina attendant's tongue clucked, then, with a rehearsed smile and feigned cheerfulness, announced, "Welcome United Airlines passengers. Currently, we welcome our pre-board passengers."

Families started making their way to the podium before she could complete the announcement. A little girl with two afro puffs waved to Alicia with her pointer finger smiling, revealing gapped teeth. Alicia mimicked the greeting just as a weary heavy-set woman unsuccessfully negotiated with a screaming toddler as they walked towards the gate. Passengers immediately turned their heads in her direction.

"What I don't understand," Dallas said. "Is why would someone want to clone my credit card and not go buck ass wild with charges?"

Alicia's curls bounced as her head went up then down. "I have been thinking about that as well. You said the only charges were small meals at local spots, right?"

"From what the bank said, yes. Nothing too large that would have even gotten my attention." He turned his head from side to side then lowered his voice. "With all the work required to raise ourselves out of poverty, get established, obtain a credit rating score above one hundred and fifteen, someone comes and just impersonates you." His rant garnered the young toddler's attention, who stuck his pacifier in the air towards Dallas as if he needed a time out.

"At this time," she said. "We welcome all Premier Platinum members, Premier Gold members, Star Alliance Gold members." Dallas removed his cell from his pocket. He and Alicia stood as the flight attendant continued squawking into the microphone.

"Premium cabin passengers including United Polaris, United First, United Business passengers." Each word lacked enthusiasm and came across as someone who'd repeated the phrase a hundred times.

"That's us," Dallas announced as he stood to his full height, waving at the generous toddler.

"Welcome aboard United Airlines, Mr. Avery." The attendant's eyes immediately brightened the moment Dallas placed his cell to the ticket scanner. Her cheeks matched the shade of her hair. The cheery mood was short-lived. The moment she saw Alicia, she was back to the previous drab demeanor. "Ma'am," she murmured as he swiped her e-ticket.

Dallas gripped Alicia's waist with his left arm, then scanned the screen a second time. "Shall we?" he said.

She rolled her hips from left to right with each step causing him to put his hand in her back pocket to keep it from falling off.

That's my baby. A little bit holy and a whole lot hood.

Chapter 11

Gang Sign

"Welcome aboard," the petite Japanese flight attendant with a short a-symmetric bob haircut greeted them as they boarded the flight.

Alicia situated herself near the window. Dallas stretched out his long legs in the aisle as soon as his bottom hit the plush leather seat. Even with the extra space allotted in First Class, it was barely enough room. "The idea of having a private jet doesn't seem like a bad idea," he said, then added, "I know what you're going to say."

"Good, then I don't have to retrieve my calculator to demonstrate how poor of an investment that would be."

Dallas removed headphones from his Messenger bag and passed Alicia a pair. He turned the dial until he located a station that played smooth jazz.

* * *

Dallas removed his headphones. "Tell me more about Patrick."

Alicia quickly looked up from the iPad she'd removed from her bag. "You want to hear about my ex-husband?" She hit the sleep button on her iPad then closed the case. "What would you like to know?"

"What drew you to him?" His question was sincere.

Alicia repositioned a curl behind her right ear. "I think what attracted me most," she said, "was his stability. I'd seen him around my grandparent's house often; he was their attorney." She slightly closed her eyes as if reviewing footage on a projector screen. "At first, I was the clumsy, chubby kid always in the way. James and I were eight when we moved in with my grandmother."

"Do you think your grandparents ever had a clue about the fortune or his real intentions?" Dallas paused before asking his next question. "He was old enough to be your father, right?"

Alicia's body stiffened, and she slowly exhaled. "With my sordid past, I think my grandmother was just excited to see me happy, at least appearing to be happy. And yes, he was much older than me."

Taking a sip of water, Dallas slowly glanced around at the other passengers seated in First Class. An older couple sat hand in hand; the wife nodded as her husband jabbered nonstop. Their silent affection was visible to even a blind person. "I witnessed my folks slowly drift away then meet again in the middle." He spoke in a low, monotone voice. "Almost as if they were MMA fighters. I can't recall when things went from bad to worse for them."

"What does anyone know about marriage?"

"Not a whole lot. I thought we'd grow out of our differences," she said.

The older gentleman seated one row up and across the aisle head bobbed so fiercely he nearly jumped out of his seat. He'd slept through all that turbulence. He quickly repositioned his comb-over then glanced around to see who'd witnessed his near fall from the seat. He partially smiled when he connected eyes with Dallas.

"Instead of looking for an exit," she continued. "I began to focus on what I could control and not on what I couldn't. I was responsible for me."

"Do you feel like you compromised?"

"You already know. You were the first to cause my toes to form a gang sign," she nudged him. "There's no need in pretending—not that I would. It is what it is. More correctly, it was. I looked for other ways we could connect since pleasurable sex was off the table, or should I say any sex."

Following a few moments of silence, Dallas said, "I can't imagine sharing a bed with you and not fulfilling your every sexual desire. Your very scent is intoxicating." The last sentence was overheard by the young businessman who walked by. He looked down at Alicia over his horn-rimmed glasses and gave her a "damn, I wish I could sample the goods" stare. She quickly averted her gaze. "See, I'm not the only one."

She elbowed him in his ribs.

"Oh, that thing is boney." He exaggeratedly rubbed the spot she touched. "I know what it's like to feel like you're pulling the weight of the entire team. Like basketball, marriage is a partnership, and there you were, footing the entire sexual bill. Did he try to overcompensate in other areas?"

Alicia opened her mouth to speak, then stopped. "I won't go into details about his anatomy. That wouldn't be proper, but I will say he was very stubborn and insecure. That's a dangerous combination for a couple of similar ages and statuses. It was disastrous for us. But still…"

"You hung in there. Not many women, especially those who possess your qualities, would remain in an unfulfilling marriage. You're a rare bird." He leaned over and kissed her on the cheek.

"We were married for twenty-three years before he passed away." She rubbed the ring finger on her left hand. "The crazy thing is, he died while in bed with someone else."

"Would you care for a cocktail?" The name tag read Ayumu.

"How is your name pronounced?" Dallas asked while mouthing the letters.

The question immediately elicited a broad smile. "Thank you for asking. It is pronounced A-you-me." Her accent was thick and posture proud.

"Just like it's spelled," said Alicia. "And what does it mean?"

"It means," she responded with a slight tilt to her head. "One who walks their own path."

"Beautiful," they said in unison.

"I'll have another, and the lady will have?" Dallas looked to Alicia.

"The same, thank you."

"Coming right up."

"You know, there's more to marriage than sex," Alicia spoke as if putting a final nail in the coffin of the conversation they began earlier.

"Shiiiit," responded a young man with locs sitting in front of them. Until that moment, he and the young blonde with tattoos covering every visible inch of her body had been silent. "Yo'," he said. "I wasn't eavesdropping," his ebony skin smooth against his full beard. "I took my headphones off for a second and heard what you said." He immediately put the noise-canceling device back on and turned his head forward. The young lady never uttered a word. "But that shit is whack. Marriage is all about knocking boots, right baby?" She turned and nodded. "You old folk don't know nothing."

"So many couples, young and old," she continued. "Place too much emphasis on one thing or another, not realizing that matrimony is like a puzzle. There're millions of little pieces that fit together to create the image. With hope, the image is of both individuals."

Dallas shifted in his seat slightly, allowing his legs more space. "My folks got it so wrong," he said, "their puzzle would look like broken glass held together with gobs of Gorilla glue."

They sipped on their drinks for a few moments as the conversations of other passengers filled the silence their thoughts created.

"Let's change the tempo," she said in a voice much lighter in pitch. "Tell me about one of the little surprises you have in store for me? If it's anything like our other excursions, I'm in for a real treat, I know."

"Tsk-tsk," the sound was accompanied by the wave of his index finger. "Can't you just be surprised?"

She batted her lashes several times, causing them to mimic butterfly wings.

With a sigh of reluctance, he said, "I won't tell everything, but I'll say, it involves a train ride and lots of wine. There, that's all I'm saying on the subject."

She quickly tapped the words on her iPad, and when he saw it, he said, "Seriously?" He removed it from her hands.

Folding her arms, she shot back, "You're no fun."

"You didn't say that last night."

"See? Why do you want to bring up grown folk's business?"

Chapter 12

Haze

Alicia awakened to find Dallas scanning his tablet.

"Good afternoon. Did anyone ever tell you that you snore?"

"I do not." She stretched as best she could while remaining in her seat.

"Snore and drool." Dallas pointed to his shirt. "There's an entire pool of drool right here with your name on it."

Her palm rubbed against the fabric. "There's nothing there. You're so horrible."

"I'm only teasing. But did you know," Dallas held up his iPad, "that trains in Germany are a popular way to travel for either business or leisure?"

Scratching an area near her nose, Alicia shook her head.

"Well, they are. And Germany's train system offers hundreds of routes and facilitates easy and convenient travel throughout Germany."

"That is impressive. How many times a day does the train go to the castle?"

"Deutsche Bahn travels directly from Munich to Neuschwanstein Castle a whopping twenty times a day."

"You've earned a Ph.D. of all things concerning the castle. I'm impressed."

Smiling, "I have a tad bit more insight. The grotto, with its small waterfalls and colorful lighting, is another—"

"Good timing," Dallas said as flight attendants began rustling in the gally preparing their dinner. Delicious aromas of cedar grilled salmon, garlic mashed potatoes, and vegetables wafted through the air. Sleeping passengers began to reposition their seats in anticipation. Crystal and china could be heard in First Class while cellophane wrappers were heard in coach. "I thought there'd be nothing left for the tour guides to share," he teased.

* * *

"Ladies and Gentlemen," the squawking of the plane's PA system instantly jarred Dallas from a nap. "We'll begin our descent into Munich Airport. Please place all trays and seats in an upright position. If you have removed any items from the overhead compartments, please return them at this time. The flight attendant will come around shortly to remove any rubbish you may have."

"Did you get any rest?" Dallas asked as she fished around the inside of her handbag. She retrieved a mint.

"There has been more news about those missing girls," he said.

Alicia's voice heavy with concern, "Mercy. What's being reported?"

"They've found at least three bodies." Scanning the screen, he said, "This isn't looking like a kidnapping for ransom."

"Is there anything tying them all together?"

Dallas spoke as if each word weighed a thousand pounds. "There's one thing they all have in common."

"And what might that be?" Alicia's voice cracked slightly.

He opened his mouth to respond when his phone alerted an incoming text from Hernandez. The police will be interviewing all individuals associated with A Place to Ponder.

"First, credit cards in our names, and now missing girls from a group that I'm a member of. This isn't looking good."

Concern filled her expression as she responded. "It's very suspicious."

* * *

The Munich airport was a visually sensual field trip. Not a scrap piece of paper could be found anywhere within the six-thousand square meters. Not a scrap piece of paper anywhere. "Can you believe close to forty-seven million people come through here on average?" she asked.

The ceiling looked like hundreds of tiny glass squares. The giant shades reminded Alicia of sailboats. Every so often, they passed a German sports car positioned throughout the building.

"You won't have to worry about the bank cutting you off," she warned him as he paused and gawked too long at a prototype BMW. "As your new financial manager, I'll cut you off at the wrists."

At the conveyor belt a few aisles over, a teenage girl appeared to be in a daze. She slightly swayed from side to side as she focused on her chewed fingernails. An older gentleman stood near the revolving suitcases. He occasionally glanced back in her direction. Her lifeless stare took in everything as passengers retrieved their belongings and headed for the exit doors. Many were greeted by loved ones or personalized signs held high by chauffeurs dressed in black and white. She knew instinctively, no one held a "Welcome, Zoe" sign. Hell, no one even knew or cared that she'd vanished from the Foster home, let alone that she'd left the United States. Zoe equally doubted she'd ever be rescued.

Chapter 13

Zoe's Story

Zoe was just eleven years old when she packed her belongings and escaped from her bedroom window. More correctly, she left the closet her foster parents called her bedroom then made her way to the room where their biological princess slept. That space was thirteen by twenty-six feet with its own gas-burning fireplace. She was foolish enough to believe this new family was the real deal. They were good. They even had the social worker fooled, but their true colors were revealed as soon as the public servant walked out.

Like many others, this family didn't select Zoe because they wanted a child to love. Instead, they had deeply rooted evil desires lurking in sinful hearts. When she wasn't the punching bag, she was where they unleashed all their deviant thoughts. At times, she felt more disgusting than a toilet.

Life seemed to have her name on every short straw drawn. That day, however, she was determined to take back her destiny. If she was going to be flat on her back, it would be by choice and not force. Either that or she would have to slit a few throats and watch folks bleed out.

When Zoe fled the previous home, the Merchandel's seemed like real friendly Christian-type people. All, "Jesus loves you," this and that. They even had the Good Book on their coffee table. That should've been another clue. Who even used a paper copy of the bible anymore? Every phone on the planet has an app for that. But she was naïve. A romantic at heart. She believed in people. That shit was about to change.

She had just cleared a height that would allow her one hundred eight-pound five-foot-two stature to shimmy through the window when the words echoed off the walls.

"What are you doing in here?" Autumn yanked the chain to a Koa wood lamp on her nightstand as she bolted upright. "Oh my God! Are you sneaking out?" Hollow orifices that housed amber eyes pierced Zoe's soul as flaming red curls bounced in every direction. "I should scream as though you're a burglar and watch my daddy come in here and blast your ass."

Not one for being punked or caught off guard, Zoe squared her shoulders, "Then why don't you fucking do it?"

With a laugh that even Lucifer would envy, "Because I don't want your mutt blood on my white carpet. What sort of half-breed are you anyway? I heard my parents saying you are Black, but you have green eyes, and your hair isn't nappy." She kicked the champagne-colored silk duvet onto the floor. "Stop standing in my face like you belong here. Who the hell do you think you are? The Queen of Sheba?"

On any other day, Zoe would've welcomed the challenge. Since the day she arrived, she had gone toe-to-toe with Autumn. That night, however, Zoe was on a mission. She had a plane to catch, and pausing long enough to remove her hoops, grab her Vaseline, and battle it out with an entitled brat wasn't in the plans.

"Listen, Bitch. I can call you by your given name, right?"

Autumn dove to her feet, searching for the pair of Chanel slippers. How anyone would pay a grand for house shoes would remain a mystery to Zoe.

"I didn't know you knew your momma's name," Autumn shot back.

Touché. Zoe had to give her that one. It was the best comeback she'd heard from the spoiled brat since the burnt-out underpaid social worker dropped her off at their front door.

"No need to scream for daddy dearest. I'm leaving and never coming back. Maybe now he'll find interest in your mommy again." Zoe relished the utter shock emanating from Autumn's face. "That is, of course, if she ever finds her face out of a bottle of Titos."

Before Autumn could retort, Zoe repositioned her backpack and slid out the window. She headed for the lights that were flashing at the end of the driveway. "Finally, my knight in shining armor," Zoe said as her left shoe touched the manicured lawn. Before her right foot could join it, she heard a blood-curling screech.

"Daddy!" Autumn barked loud enough for neighbors to switch on their lights. "Someone's trying to break in through my bedroom window." Her screams would have easily won an Academy Award. "They're going to rape me."

Zoe reached the passenger side of the car just as the floodlights came on, chasing away all the safety of the darkness.

That night, Zoe escaped. Unfortunately, she'd learn, not all knights in shining armor come to protect. Some come to imprison.

Chapter 14

Cobblestone Roads

Although Alicia had traveled the globe, there was something magical about being in Germany. Stepping onto the ancient cobblestone roads instantly teleported her to times gone by. Before the modern conveniences of electricity, running water, and gas-powered automobiles, she imagined a medieval life where times were simpler. She twirled in place with her eyes closed and arms wide open, emulating the miniature figurine once permanently confined within a younger Alicia's painted musical box.

It dawned on her the improbability that a stone-paved road that welcomed countless travelers from around the planet could still exist in such unspoiled condition. "Each cobblestone looks as if it was just placed," she said while viewing tiny partially timbered homes ornated with window flower boxes containing beautifully colored flowers. "Look around. The city is pristine. There isn't a piece of litter anywhere."

Passersby looked their way. Many whispered and pointed at Dallas. Evidentially, his stardom reached lands beyond America's shores.

"Would you prefer to travel by train or rental?" Dallas' question brought her back to modern times.

Embracing him, she said, "Let's take a train to the castle then the car for a ride along the Romantic Road."

Dallas placed both hands squarely on his hips and inquired, "Who said we're going on the Romantic Road?"

"So that was your surprise, she said, beaming. You couldn't visit this part of Germany and not take the three-day journey along the Romantic Road." She turned to him and then said, "What if we do the rental first, then ride the train back?"

"I like that idea. The rental company is close by. But first, let's grab lunch before we go." Dallas patted his stomach. "I believe you're going to be thrilled with the place I've selected for us to eat."

"Is it as good as your peanut butter and jelly sandwich?"

"Nothing, Ms. Mitchell, and I do mean nothing," he overly enunciated the last word, "is as good as my peanut butter and jelly sandwich."

A gigantic elephant's head was suspended above the stucco-walled entrance to Restaurant Savanna Munich. The tusks and trunk faced up towards the heavens. As they walked through the door, a brightly lit, well stocked bar came into view. An enormous sign in Rasta colors of green, red, and yellow read, What's NOT on the menu.

"Mr. Avery?" the well-endowed waitress beamed as soon as she took a gander at Dallas. "Welcome back. It's wonderful seeing you twice in one week." Her cocoa skin glowed as though kissed by the sun. The form-fitting, leopard print, one-shoulder dress had a slight bump just above the waist beads. Each time her arm moved; the copper bangles chimed. Miniature conch shells adorned her shoulder length locs. "Will your daughter also be joining you?" The accent was rich with a mixture of the Mother Land and bratwurst and sauerkraut.

"What did you just ask me?" Dallas snapped.

Beads of sweat formed on her upper lip, "I...I was asking if your daughter will be joining you as well?"

"There must be some mistake," he said. "I don't have a daughter, and I have never been here before today."

"You know what they say, Sir? We all have a twin. Yours happened to have been here a few days ago." Her shoulders relaxed. "Will it be the two of you?"

"Yes, just the two of us," Alicia answered, giving Dallas' hand a squeeze.

"Wonderful. Follow me, please."

Soft white light shone through the openings for the eyes and mouth of the mask overlooking the table. Zebra-print oversized pillows were propped against the bright orange walls. The hostess placed two menus before them and said, "Your waitress will be with you momentarily. Enjoy your meal." She sashayed back to the main entrance to greet the next guest.

"Can you imagine," Alicia said, "that from our humble beginnings, we would one day afford to jet-set around the planet?"

"There is something to be said of hard work, determination, and grit."

"Grit. That's a word younger people don't seem to grasp. Having fortitude and resilience is critical to life not just success."

Alicia opened the menu. "Everything sounds delicious. I don't know if I want to be adventurous and dive right into the zebra, crocodile, or black tiger prawns."

As she spoke, the waitress came to the table. Her dress was designed similarly to the hostess but with a cougar pattern. Her locs were thicker and wrapped in a crown-like fashion. She looked to be slightly older than their hostess. Words flowed from her lips like honey dripping from the comb. "Hello, my name is Oy'a." Alicia and Dallas leaned towards her as she spoke. "I will be serving you today. Might I start you off with a cocktail?"

"What wine would you suggest?" Dallas asked while still viewing the menu, but his brow wrinkled as though still pondering the hostess's words.

"The Navigator is a favorite. It is a shiraz from the southernmost wine-growing region of South Africa. It's a sensual mixture of clove, elderberry, vanilla, fig, white pepper, peaches, and other flowers, berries, and spices."

"That sounds delicious," Alicia chimed in.

"Bring us a bottle, please. We haven't yet decided on our order."

"Right away, Sir."

Alicia closed her menu and asked, "Has Adrian texted any new updates?"

Dallas retrieved his cell from his pocket, punched in his code, then scrolled down. "Nope. Nothing further."

"Maybe no news is good news."

Before he might respond, Oy'a returned. "Have you decided upon your meal, Sir?"

"We have indeed. We'll have the Exotic plate," Dallas said with a slight grin.

"Brave, are we?"

Alicia immediately scanned the menu. Her mouth opened wide as she read the selection, "Zebra loin, crocodile fillet steak, Namibian beef fillet steak, leaf salad…monkey glands." She looked up at Dallas and Oy'a. "You only live, once right?"

"Wrong," Dallas said. "You only die once."

* * *

Zoe woke to find her clothes entirely removed and her mouth as dry as the Sahara. Her head ached as she tried to lift it from the pillow. The last thing she recalled was standing at the conveyor belt, waiting for her Daddy, as she was forced to call him, to retrieve their luggage.

She'd met him on social media. He commented on her videos at first randomly, then daily. He later began to inbox her on Instagram, and they started a relationship. His smile captured her heart. She'd never use the word love, but her pulse raced, and her heart skipped a beat when he said her name. After three months or so, Zoe divulged her secrets of the abuse she'd been enduring starting at home with her crackhead mom, then in many of the foster homes.

"We have a program designed to help young girls such as yourself," he said. "We have everything arranged, homeschooling, work-study, and a stipend. You even get to travel. We're going to Munich, Germany, soon to visit a famous castle."

"A castle?" Zoe's disposition immediately shifted. "A real castle?"

"As real as they get. There're no damsels in distress or dragons," he said, then added. "I have one more surprise. That's even better than any fire-breathing reptile" His smile beamed. "You're my daughter, my flesh and blood."

Zoe glanced around at the windowless, eight by ten-foot closet her newest Foster family had placed her in. It was far from the beautifully decorated room they displayed for the case manager; they always lie. "When can we leave?"

* * *

The sign on the wall read Burg-Hotel. Although the room was fancier than the dump, she had called a bedroom, the abuse was at an altogether different level. The only saving grace, for now, was that she was drugged much of the time. She stopped her mind from going into overdrive, thinking of what untold horrors took place to cause the bruises alongside her wrists, inner thighs, midriff, and ankles.

The water from the shower stopped. The door opened as steam escaped the bathroom. Zoe quickly closed her eyes and pretended to be asleep. She cracked her eyelids open enough to see a stranger exit with a towel wrapped around his waist. He reminded her of Fat Bastard from the movie Austin Powers: The Spy Who Shagged Me. The thought of his body coming within a foot of hers nearly caused her to vomit.

"Berndt, my man," Daddy said as he came into the room holding two disposable cups with coffee. "I hope she was to your satisfaction."

"Ja." His German accent was thick. "She was perfect. Only next time, not too many tranquilizers. I would like a little movement. But no fighters. I am not good with the fighters."

"Absolutely," Daddy agreed. "I have new merchandise arriving next week. I'll be sure to call you first. You're my most loyal customer."

Berndt dressed, put a wad of Euros on the counter then left.

Moments later, Zoe was yanked by a waft of hair and snatched to her feet. "That Sleeping Beauty act may have worked for that old fart, but don't think I was the slightest bit fooled."

Whatever he had given her prevented her from fighting back as she was dragged into the bathroom and thrust under the full blast shower head. She wouldn't give him the satisfaction of seeing her cry. She couldn't anyway. Zoe long ago lost the ability to shed a tear. All allotted tears fell before she stopped wearing diapers. What Zoe was doing, however, was developing a plan of escape. That she knew how to do very well.

Chapter 15

Not Cinderella

Dallas and Alicia waited at the car rental counter for only a few moments. "Everything done in Germany seems to be done efficiently," he said as he scanned the room and saw antique artifacts positioned throughout the space.

"Grosse Gott, willkommen bei der Autovermietung. Sprichst du Deutsch?" The young lady at the counter nametag read Sabine. She was a beautiful mixture of German, Italian, and Polish descent. The short-cropped haircut accentuated her unusual colored eyes. Every fleck of green, amber, and violet danced as she spoke.

"Ich spreche ein bisschen deutsch," Alicia answered. But I prefer English."

"Very well. What brand automobile might you desire to rent today?" She directed her brilliant white smile towards Dallas.

Having the opportunity to travel at breakneck speeds down the autobahn nearly made him giddy. "As much as I'd love to experience the wind whizzing through my hair —"

Alicia exaggeratedly cleared her throat.

"As I was saying," he continued. "I'd love to drive one hundred twenty miles an hour down the Autobahn, but my six-foot seven-inch legs simply won't allow it."

"Might we suggest the Mercedes E Class Wagon? It provides ample legroom and space for your luggage while providing breakneck speeds, as you say."

"That would be perfect."

Tapping a few keys, she looked up and added, "There seems to be a problem with your card, Sir."

Dallas stepped forward. "My apologies. Please try this one?"

With each card, she gave the same response, "I am sorry, Sir. Your card has declined the charge."

"This is quite embarrassing. I was the subject of identity theft. My bank must have frozen my cards as a measure of precaution. Do you accept American currency?" he asked, reaching a hand into his pocket.

"I am sorry to hear of the issues with your bank, Sir. However, we are unable to accept cash," she said.

"Here, you may use this card," Alicia stepped up to the counter.

She swiped Alicia's card then returned it to her. "There is an added benefit to the vehicle you have selected," she said. "It has been retrofitted with an additional safety feature. It is completely bulletproof. The vehicle was previously used to chauffeur dignitaries. As you may imagine, some politicians and royals are overly cautious. That will not be a problem, will it?"

"No problem at all," Dallas replied.

"Perfect. There is no additional fee, of course." She tapped a few keys on the computer, and a small stack of forms spilled out.

After signing several pages, Dallas placed their luggage safely in the oversized trunk.

"First stop," Dallas announced as they pulled off the lot. "Is to take my Queen to see a castle."

The nearly two-hour drive along the countryside was breathtakingly spectacular. For time's sake, Dallas drove a combination of two-lane roads and highways that would've made Nascar drivers envious. Riding on the passenger side was like being in a moving museum. For the first time in a very long time, Alicia was near speechless. Every so often, Dallas would glance over and smile. Her face glowed like a child at Christmastime. The vision of her sitting there fully immersed in the experience he provided caused his heart to swell with pride.

Upon arrival, they began "touristing" right away by taking a stroll around the pastel-colored town of Füssen, taking selfies in front of the castle's gates and spires.

As they strolled the suspended bridge hundreds of feet above the babbling brook, bystanders remarked about the exquisiteness of the surroundings. Several spectators never ventured beyond the center of the bridge. The more daring ones peeked over the edge as though simply overlooking a second-story balcony. Holding onto Dallas' hand, Alicia quickly glanced. "Okay, one look is sufficient."

Dallas laughed as he boldly lingered and enjoyed the sights of the waterfalls and those parasailing through the air.

"Can you imagine dedicating and investing twenty-four years in building a castle as beautiful as this, and never truly getting to call it home?" He checked his phone for messages.

"King Ludwig II and his psychiatrist mysteriously drowned mere days after the king was declared insane. Six weeks later, this gorgeous place was opened to the public," she said.

Braving one final glance over the edge of the bridge, Alicia said, "Neuschwanstein literally means 'New Swan Castle.' She pointed down to the flock of swans basking in the sun. "The irony of it all. He thought he was the 'Swan Knight.'"

A group of tourists walked onto the bridge, eyeing Dallas with suspicion. "While Neuschwanstein's look is that of a medieval castle," they overheard the guide saying. "It was equipped inside with state-of-the-art technology at that time. For example, on every floor of the castle, there were toilets with automatic flushing systems, as well as an air heating system for the whole castle."

Alicia and Dallas continued walking towards the majestic castle. She marveled at the gorgeous landscaping and artificial cave. "I wonder if I might be able to hire a landscaper to replicate this when I return home to Chicago?"

When Alicia said the word Chicago, Dallas opened his mouth, then stopped. He then said, "I'm certain you can. They have castles there, too. In fact, ..."

Neuschwanstein's interior was as majestic as its outside. Only fourteen rooms were completed before Ludwig II's sudden death in 1886, yet they were majestically decorated. The two-story throne room was designed in Byzantine style, with wall paintings depicting angels. Ironically, there was no throne in the Throne Room. The stately images, hand-honed stonework, ornate carvings, and lush tapestries were a visual vacation. Alicia said, "Even without being able to take photos, this experience will forever be in my heart. This is the most marvelous gift I've ever received." She stood on her tiptoes and planted a kiss on Dallas' right cheek. "Thank you, this was absolutely perfect."

"I accept your gratitude, but our trip is far from over. We have plenty of sightseeing left to do and a few hotel rooms that require our ... special touch. Next stop, Burg-Hotel."

Chapter 16

It Takes a Village

"Let's stop along the way and visit a few villages," Alicia suggested as they got into the rental to drive the one hundred and fifty miles between Füssen and Rothenburg ob der Tauber.

"That sounds like an awesome plan. Where would you like to stop first?" Dallas asked as he put on his seatbelt.

Alicia swiped a few times on her screen. "Augsburg is Bavaria's oldest city. There is a great bakery," she said. "They have hundreds of five-star reviews for the coffee and pastries.

"I'm always up to eating pastries," said Dallas as he tapped his stomach.

After the brief stop, they were back on B17, heading towards A7. "I believe I could be right at home in Germany," Alicia said as they passed quaint picturesque communities. Each had a church in the center of town. "Life seems to go at a slower pace."

Just then a low whirl turned into a high-pitch whizz as an Audi sped past on their left. The downdraft caused the rental to swerve slightly to the right. "You were saying?" Dallas asked.

"That car went by so fast, I could barely make out the color, make, or model," she let out a slow whistle. "Life may move slowly, but cars travel at the speed of light."

"Umm um," she remarked. "Their driving might appear reckless, but the lifestyle is very laid back. Have you noticed how welcoming everyone has been so far?"

"A train would have gotten us there in the same amount of time," Dallas said. "But driving gives us an up-close and personal experience."

"Maybe next time," she said. "We have photos and memories to last a lifetime." She swiped several times on the screen.

Turning the phone towards Dallas. "This looks like fun. Do you think we might have time to stop at Fuggerei?" she asked, meaning the walled Roman Catholic housing complex for the poor built in the early 1500s by Jakob Fugger.

"I read about that place," he said. "It still serves as subsidized housing to this day. They offer tours, but we may not have enough time for that."

Children riding in a BMW waved as they exited the highway. Alicia waved back. "Just a drive-by is all I need. Perhaps when we return, we can swing by Harburg Castle and stay overnight in Dinkelsbühl."

"I love that you're already planning our future," he said, grinning.

That caused Alicia to chuckle out loud. She had to admit, she was enjoying traveling with him. Things looked different when viewing them in his presence.

Dallas' phone rang. "I forgot to synch it to the car," he said, then passed it to Alicia.

"Hello. Yes, he's here. Let me put you on speaker." Alicia tapped a few keys and Hernandez's voice bellowed.

"Hey, I know you're on vacation," Adrian said. "But I had to update you."

"Is this about the girls?" Dallas hit the button to raise the windows to hear better.

"Man, you're not going to believe it. These fools hired people who looked like us to lure the girls into captivity."

Alicia's chin tucked as her eyes bulged. "How'd they find out?"

"A valet who wants to one day be a journalist has been taking photos of them. She had pictures of them with the girls and of their cars." Hernandez paused to let his words register with them. "They even had fake license plates."

"With the endorsement deals, it wasn't too hard to figure out at least one of the cars we drove." Dallas's complexion paled, and his right eye twitched. His breathing labored as he gripped the steering wheel so tightly, his knuckles cracked.

"Exactly. Mark was out with one of the officers and saw a car exactly like his with the same plate. He thought the car was stolen, so he called it into the police."

"Talk about being at the right place at the right time," Alicia chimed in while Dallas nodded.

"You know him. He wasn't going to wait on the cops, so he followed the guy. By the time the police arrived, he had already watched him knock on a door, and he said he almost fainted."

Dallas pulled the car onto the shoulder of the road so he could focus. "What did he see?"

"Himself. Well, someone who had a striking resemblance." Hernandez whistled. "Worse, the police chief was involved. They caught him. Get this, he had one of the girls."

"This explains the credit cards as well," Alicia said, shaking her head.

Cars sped down the autobahn on their way to locations unknown. Life was passing by as usual for some while it was falling apart for others.

"I bet the news is eating this up," Dallas mused. "Did they find my doppelganger?"

"That's why I'm calling you," he said. "It seems that the valet overheard you, I mean him, telling the girl he was taking her to Cinderella's castle."

* * *

Zoe sat with her face to the window nursing her bruised eye and swollen lip. She refused to look one more moment at the man she once thought was her rescuer. She questioned how she would escape. Although offered German in middle-high school, she never took classes, yet one more stupid decision came to haunt her.

As Daddy snored, she saw a Mercedes pull into the parking lot. The driver was so tall, that he looked as if he would tower most men even from up high. He walked over to the passenger side and opened the door for a beautiful woman. Now, that is what a gentleman does.

Her breath caught in her chest. It couldn't be. His height and the way he moved, she thought she would faint. If that was Dallas Avery, then who was the man she'd been calling Daddy?

Zoe knew what needed to be done. She whispered a prayer that God would give her strength, protection, and wisdom.

* * *

The check-in counter of the Burg-Hotel was like being in another fairytale. Set in a 12th-Century building, it offered spa facilities and elegant rooms overlooking gardens and the beautiful Tauber Valley. It was situated on the edge of Rothenburg's Medieval town center. A male nearly walked into the glass doors gawking at Dallas. Alicia was about to comment on it, when the concierge came through a side door.

He ogled Dallas as he spoke, "Welcome, Mr. Avery?" His words sounded more like a question than a statement. "Do you require an additional room?"

"We will not need two rooms." Alicia draped Dallas and offered her credit card.

"Danke, Frau," he glanced at the Visa Black card. "Frau Mitchell."

After tapping a few keys on the computer, the printer spit out a small stack of forms.

"All of our rooms have a seating area, mini-bar, and cable television," said the blonde concierge, adjusting wire-rimmed glasses. "We have a suite available with a king-size bed and separate lounge area. It overlooks the valley."

"That will be perfectly fine," Dallas said.

Still awkwardly staring, Alicia asked, "Sir, is there something the matter? You seem to be a bit preoccupied."

Startled at the tone, he adjusted his lapel and straightened his tie, "My apologies, Ma'am. It seems lately we … have had men who look like, how do you say in America? Basketball players."

Dallas quickly turned to Alicia then shook his head as if clearing out an awkward thought. "Is there anything further we should know about the room?"

"It comes with a complimentary breakfast," his voice slightly back to normal. "It is delicious. We encourage our patrons to dine in the restaurant. It has a rose garden and terrace."

"That sounds delightful." Alicia said as she watched several guests walk towards the pool with thick luscious white towels in their hands.

"And our spa area includes a sauna, spa, showers, and a relaxation area. We also have private two-hour sessions." He said the word private as though it was a naughty word.

Dallas signed for the room, including the spa package, and accepted the key.

"One final thing," he added. "That archway leads into the old Dominican monastery's gardens. Guests are welcome to relax here."

"Thank you so very much," he waved for an attendant to assist with their luggage. "Enjoy your evening." Dallas and Alicia walked behind the concierge as he led them to their room. The suitcases left indentations on the carpeted floors.

"I don't know if I'm imagining that people are acting a bit odd," Alicia said. "Or if it just an overactive imagination based on the current events." The young man swiped the key to unlock the door. Dallas reached into his pocket for Euro for a tip.

Their room was on the first floor. Alicia nearly gasped at the beautiful décor of the room which was like a miniature castle.

"Germans have a phenomenal way with decorations," she said. "I'm taking mental notes."

"Indeed, they do," Dallas responded. "Would you care to join me in the badezimmer?"

The bathroom was a designer's dream. Hand-painted marble tiles lined the floors and walls. Extending as high as the crown molding. Stunning fixtures looked more like works of art than sources for water. The room supplied thick, thirsty towels and matching bathrobes.

A bottle of wine was in a bucket of ice near the sienna four-poster bed. The white lace canopy and oval archway provided the backdrop for a night of unbridled passion.

Alicia lay with her head on Dallas' chest, their hands intertwined. His other hand played with her curls as they fell across his shoulder.

"This was the most unforgettable day of my life. It was like living a fairytale."

"I am so glad you enjoyed it."

"My heart aches for those young girls and their families. My brother and I were in the system. It can be more brutal than words can describe." She paused to steady her voice. "At times, it is like being in a perpetual cycle of abuse."

"Had it not been for one overly zealous valet, we might never have gotten to the bottom of this," he said, staring at the ceiling. "Tomorrow, I will contact the police to get an update and find out what I can do to assist."

"I love the way you seek to make a difference in the lives of people. You are such a generous soul." She wrapped her arms around his neck. "I am thankful to have you in my life."

Their lovemaking was sweet and passionate. The earth didn't shake, thunder didn't erupt from the atmosphere, there was no tsunami downpour. Yet that night, their souls tied in a way that Heaven took notice.

They became one.

Chapter 14

Escape

Alicia sat upright in bed and adjusted her eyes to view the clock positioned on the nightstand. It read 01:23. She wasn't sure what caused her to awaken. She reached for her telephone and realized it wasn't there. Gently moving Dallas' arm from her waist, she stood to look on the coffee table.

"Hey, is everything okay?" Dallas rubbed his eyes. "What time is it?"

"I didn't mean to wake you. I'm not certain what's going on. I feel like someone is calling me."

"Did you hear the phone ring?" Dallas stretched his entire body while still lying in bed.

"I didn't hear a phone; I felt the call." She moved a few items from the counter. "I can't seem to find my phone. Perhaps it's still in the car."

"I'll go and check for you. Be back in a jiffy." He slipped on his jeans and t-shirt and grabbed the keys, then headed out the door.

Alicia recognized the feeling. The same sense of dread overwhelmed and threatened to consume her eight-year-old self. Alicia now realized, she also had a feeling of doom, when she first married. The last time she felt such urgency was in Scotland.

She quickly dressed and packed their items. She was zipping the luggage when Dallas rushed into the room.

"We have to leave, now!" His eyes widened at the sight of her standing there fully clothed, and bags packed. "How did you—"

Chapter 18

Awakened

"Somethings not right," Daddy clumsily awakened from his stupor. "It's too damn quiet in here." Rubbing the sleep from his eyes, he staggered to the bathroom, the closet, then looked under the bed. Scratching his head, he yelled, "How the fu—?"

Before he might finish his sentence, his head snaps in the direction of the vanity near the door. He bolts to the table, hysterically tossing items in the air. "My wallet is missing. She took my damn wallet," he shouted as items crashed onto the floor.

Daddy's feet thudded across the carpet as he stomped in the direction of the door. He hesitated long enough to snatch a pair of jeans and a jacket from the back of the chair. He nearly toppled over onto the table, reaching for his shoes.

He jammed his hands into the inner pocket of the coat, he croaked,

"Well, Dad. At least your drunk ass taught me one good thing." He said, pulling a spare key and a wad of cash from the inside of the jacket pocket. "Who knew your bullshit advise would come in handy." He didn't bother to put on shoes or pants before snatching open the door into the narrow hallway.

Daddy stood silent for a moment. She just might be stupid enough to run to a nearby room. All he heard were the ear-piercing screams of a crying baby followed by a female speaking in German. He raised his fist above the door then brought it back down to his side. He had more pressing issues than an unruly child.

He whacked the elevator button several times and nearly fell backward as he maneuvered his feet into the pant legs. Just as he was about to bolt towards the door leading to the stairs, the elevator door opened.

The elevator suddenly stopped on the next floor as he was maneuvering his long legs into the pants. Daddy stuck his head out just as he zipped the fly. The dimly lit hallway was eerily desolate. He nearly pulverized the button to shut the doors, then stuffed both feet into the shoes. Again, the elevator stopped. This time, his head banged against the wall. Rather than take the chance it would stop again, he sprinted to the exit door then dashed down the remaining flight of stairs.

Daddy burst through the atrium door to see the elevator going up to the top floors. As he was about to dash back up the stairs, something caught his eye. Several figures ran towards the parking lot.

He thrust his hands into his jacket pocket. "Shit." He patted several other pockets and cursed again.

Outside, he squinted until his eyes adjusted to the darkness. He took off running when he heard the first door slam. Then another. And finally, a third. Daddy did a one-eighty just as a black Mercedes sped out of the parking lot. Although dark outside, he recognized the driver, "Dallas," droplets of spittle fell onto his lapel as he uttered the name.

His long legs dashed across the parking lot in no time. Within minutes, he was behind the wheel of a rental car. Daddy slammed his foot on the brake pedal, he hit the start button. "You can run," he shouted at the top of his lungs. "But you can't hide."

* * *

"Are we safe?" A timid voice came from the backseat. Alicia nearly jumped out of her seatbelt.

"Jez, you scared the life out of me," she turned her head to get a closer look. "Who are you?" Before she could answer, Alicia switched on the overhead light. "I feel like I already know you. Did you call out to me?" she asked.

Tears filled Zoe's eyes and rolled down her youthful cheeks. "You felt me?" Her sobs became uncontrollable. "I haven't cried since I was a baby," she said, practically smacking herself in the face to swipe at the tears.

"I most certainly did." Alicia quickly reached into her bag to retrieve some Kleenex. "You're safe now." She passed her a wad of tissues.

"Put on your seatbelts, now," Dallas barked. The Mercedes' front tires nearly came off the pavement.

Zoe snatched her belt so forcefully, it locked. Hands shaking, she released it and pulled it again. This time slower, and then it clicked into place.

Dallas quickly turned off the autobahn. "Zoe," he said in a softer tone. "Tell Alicia what you shared with me."

"I was kidnapped and brought here," she said.

"By whom?" Alicia asked.

"At first, I thought it was a dream come true," Zoe said. "I was living a fairytale. You know," she blew her nose. "Like Cinderella."

"Then what happened?" Alicia put her hand out to collect the used tissue. Zoe reached and held her hand tightly.

Dallas passed Alicia his phone, "Punch in the passcode," he yelled. "Please, bring up the GPS. I have a feeling we are going to need it." Alicia did as he asked.

"You don't sound German," Alicia said. "Where're you originally from?"

"I live in Texas with a Foster family. I received an invitation for a banquet and responded right away." She stopped speaking and dropped her chin to her chest. "I should have known it was all too good to be true. Who would've wanted to claim me as their child?" she said. "My own mother left me on the side of the road."

From the backseat, Zoe told them how she'd come to be in the same hotel as them. She shared how she thought she was going abroad to go to school as an exchange student. Zoe then abruptly stopped talking.

"You have nothing to feel guilty about," Dallas broke the silence. "You and the other girls were preyed upon and tricked."

"I knew he, wasn't you?" she said as she squared her shoulders.

"How'd you know?" Dallas asked as he glanced in the rearview mirror.

"He ordered shellfish and seafood." She lifted her chin. "I read your article in GQ. He didn't tip the waitress," she said in a low voice. "And he got majorly pissed off when people asked for pictures or an autograph."

"That was very observant of you," said Alicia mustering all her strength to sound calm even though her foot tapped feverishly on the floorboard.

The car swerved to the left, nearly throwing Alicia onto Dallas' lap. Zoe clutched her necklace and yelled.

Dallas weaved between cars like an Indie racecar driver. He glimpsed multiple times into the rearview mirror.

"Did you try calling the police?" Alicia asked Zoe.

She craned her neck to look at the cars following behind. She saw the bright lights of a fast-approaching vehicle. "I didn't. He had all the phones," she said. "Is that him?"

Alicia looked in the side-view mirror and tapped Dallas' leg. "Did you buckle your seatbelt?" Her voice was commanding and strong. Not at all like Zoe's trembling, cracking cadence.

Zoe eased up her head a few inches, jerking it fully back down before glancing again. "That's Daddy," she screamed. "That's him. Oh, Jesus. Oh, Jesus."

Chapter 19

Trust No One

"Don't panic," Dallas told her. "It's not him." A middle-aged lady with teased hair in an updo zipped by as if they were standing still.

"I was scared to call the police," Zoe said. "Because the bastard who he let attack me this morning had on a badge."

"Are you positive that it was a badge?" asked Dallas.

"He didn't think I saw it, but I did," tears again filled her eyes. "When he opened his wallet to pay, the light reflected off it, and I saw it clearly.

"So much for involving the local authorities," he said. "We can't be certain who we can trust."

Alicia scratched a mole on her arm until it turned bright red. Dallas eased a hand over hers. "Hit speed dial one," he said.

After a few short rings, "Hey, brother. What's up?"

"We have an additional passenger with us," he said.

"Are they injured?" His voice was more alert than when he initially answered.

"Not in the way that you mean. It's Zoe, one of the missing girls." Dallas informed him of the situation.

They heard a faint dial tone followed by a phone ringing. "I'm on it," said Hernandez.

"Marhaba ya Siddiqui," the voice sounded friendly.

"What language is that?" Alicia inquired of Dallas.

He listened a few moments more, "Arabic, I think," he said.

Dallas exited the highway and pulled the car to a stop between two buildings. He left the engine running but turned off the lights.

Zoe frantically looked from side to side as she shifted in the seat.

* * *

Three minutes later, Hernandez ended the second call. "We're all set," he said. "How much gas do you have?"

Dallas looked at the dashboard, "I have a full tank."

"Perfect." A light came on in the building to their right, and Zoe screamed so loudly, Hernandez dropped his phone. Alicia and Dallas both jumped.

"Can you have someone on the scene soon?" Dallas placed the car in gear and took an exit leading up a ramp.

"The police are in on it," Zoe yelled. "At least the German ones are."

Alicia tried to quiet her down. "Adrian, the police are his customers."

"Oh shit," he said, dialing the other phone. "Hang tight."

Dallas again pulled the car to a sudden stop. This time, behind a building. Cars zoomed by on the highway, but no one came near. He took out his phone and pinged the coordinates to Hernandez.

"Zoe, you're safe with us. What made you get into this car?" The question seemed to help the youth settle down. She took a deep breath before responding.

"I watched when you pulled up to the hotel. I saw Mr. Avery as he walked around to open your door," she said. "The way you smiled at him, then him kissing you. It was the most romantic thing I'd ever seen in my life." For the second time, she cried.

They allowed her tears to flow until her chest heaved, and she stopped. Alicia passed her the package of tissues. "Listen, things might get a bit hectic, so I need you to stay focused and do exactly as we tell you, okay?" he said in a stern voice. "No second-guessing. You understand me?"

Zoe nodded and blew her nose again.

Dallas put the car in drive and navigated through the small town.

"I know what his real name is."

Both Dallas and Alicia whipped their heads in her direction.

"It's Shahid." He had it engraved on the back of his watch. "Shahid McPherson."

* * *

Shahid punched the redial button on his phone.

"What're you doing calling me at this hour of the morning?" The voice nearly inaudible.

"We have a problem?"

"What do you mean, we?" A bed creaked several times. "Don't you mean you have a problem?" Heavy footsteps sounded as he spoke.

Exhaling deeply. "I said what I meant," Shahid countered. "Zoe's escaped."

Profanity in both English and German erupted from the receiver. "What do you mean, escaped?"

A female's voice sounded in the background. "Zurück schlafen gehen," she whispered in a raspy voice.

"I will, dear. You go back to sleep as well."

Shahid wished he could be in his bed resting.

"Let me guess, instead of taking care of the problem, you were celebrating with…what is it that you Americans like to splurge on? Louis XIII Magnum."

"I wasn't drunk—"

"Bull shit."

"I don't have time to argue," he switched lanes and took a hard left-hand turn to exit the highway. "She must have put something in my food. I was sitting there one minute, then passed out the next."

"You were outsmarted by a measly child?" The laugh was followed by a series of gagging coughs. "Whatever the issue," he continued after catching his breath. "You have to handle it on your own. I will not be implicated in this. The mere mention of my name, and it will be the very last thing you do." With that, he hit the end call button, and the phone went silent. Shahid hit redial, but it immediately went to voicemail.

"How? What? You blocked me, you fat bastard?" Shahid yelled as the voicemail captured his call. He smashed the end call button so hard, his finger cracked.

Thanks to Berndt, his passport, ID, and name were all fake. If he played his cards right, he could be out of the country before anyone realized he was an impostor, or that his name was Shahid McPherson.

He had one final loose end to tie up, then he could vanish. Pressing a few keys on his phone, and a map appeared with a blue blinking dot. Opening the side compartment on the door, he took out an M5. Punching the gas pedal, he aimed to take care of the problem.

Chapter 20

Hidden in Plain Sight

"How could I have been so dumb to think someone would love me?" she said twirling, the necklace between her fingers.

"Zoe, I know this is hard to understand," Alicia said. "But this isn't your fault."

An older man with a vintage truck that could have been displayed in a museum hauled hay along the narrow street. He was in no hurry at all.

"He even gave me this stupid thing." Zoe snatched the necklace from her neck.

Alicia quickly turned to Dallas just as he reached back to grab it. "Who gave this to you?" he asked.

Terror filled her response. "Daddy, I mean, Shahid."

"Do you think it's sending a signal back?" Alicia asked. Her eyes darting from left to right.

"Shit. We can't be certain." Dallas smashed it on the console with the edge of his phone, then sped off. He lowered the driver's side window and threw the broken pieces down into a ravine. "We have to get moving and fast."

* * *

Shahid tapped the screen of his cell. The blue light suddenly stopped blinking. A string of profanity exited his lips just as a car sped past him. He watched the driver's side window go down just enough to watch a hand toss out something. "Gotcha." His car reached the side of theirs so quickly, Dallas had no time to react.

"Duck!" he yelled as the car was hit by dozens of metal objects followed by sparks of fire.

Zoe screamed from the backseat as she fell to the floor, holding her hands over her head as more bullets peppered the Mercedes. Dallas jerked the steering wheel to the right, and the car cascaded down the side of the hill. Dust from the dirt road filled the air like smoke from Mount Saint Hellen.

Shahid smacked his hands along the steering wheel as he let out a loud whooping sound. The truck carrying the hay came around the corner, nearly colliding with Shahid. He then slammed on the breaks, causing the vehicle to spin around. He immediately hit the accelerator and sped off.

* * *

"Is everyone alright?" Dallas asked moving, his neck from side to side.

"Wait?" Zoe stammered. "How're we still alive?" She checked every inch of her body. "Am I dreaming? Are we dead?"

Grabbing the slash across her neck and chest caused by the edge of the strap, Alicia answered, "No."

"I'm confused," said Zoe. "Did I imagine the gunshots?"

Dallas unbuckled his seatbelt then lowered his window. After a few moments, he opened the door and stepped out. "This is one upgrade I'm eternally thankful for," he said, as he walked around the car.

Alicia used a tissue to dabble the blood droplets on her blouse. "We didn't request it," she said.

Dallas glanced down at Alicia. "How badly are you hurt?" he said.

"You got hit?" squealed Zoe.

Fishing out Band-Aids from her purse, she applied several to stop the bleeding. "No, I'm fine. We all are fine."

"You mean, this car is bulletproof—?" Her mouth remained open for several seconds. "Dang, ya'll be rolling like that?"

Something about the way the sentence came out caused everyone to laugh. Soon it was hysteria, until Dallas' phone rang.

"I have a friend on his way. You'll remember him," Hernandez announced through the speaker. "He's the pilot I sent to Scotland." Dallas waived off any comments from the backseat. "Do you have all of your identifications?"

Zoe nodded, "I snatched it before I left the hotel room."

"Dallas," Hernandez said. "The pilot says Rothenburg Gorlitz Airport is near you. I'm sending the coordinates now. Get there as quickly as possible," he added. "Someone has reported hearing gunshots in a small community. German police are on the way to the scene."

"Thank you, Man," Dallas choked up slightly, "We're heading there now. See you soon."

Chapter 21

No Place Like Home

Zoe's turned over beneath the blanket as the jet hit slight turbulence. She returned to the fetal position as Alicia tucked the covers around her small frame. "How are you doing?" she asked Dallas as she repositioned beside him.

He placed his arm behind her waist and slid her closer to him, then covered her lips with a passionate kiss. She embraced him tightly. A tear ran down her cheek and landed on his. Drawing back, he asked, "Are you okay?"

"I thought when we left Scotland, I left the chaos behind," she said. "I guess no matter where I go, madness has a way of finding me." She paused before continuing. "My grandmother used to say, 'Baby, life ain't easy. We must do the best we can, with what we have, where we are.'"

She placed her head on his chest. His words reverberated through his jacket. "That is priceless advice."

"Would you care for refreshments," asked the attendant as she shifted her blonde tresses behind her ear. The name tag read Heidi.

"I will have sparkling water," said Alicia.

Dallas shook his head. "Nothing for me."

Heidi's blue eyes gazed towards Zoe. "We are letting her rest for now," Alicia answered the unasked question.

"Hernandez called while you were resting," he said. "They arrested Shahid as he tried to board a flight to the US."

"That is comforting to hear."

"He squealed like a stuffed pig. He dimed out everyone involved at the first mention of a deal. He even drew maps to the locations of all the houses where the girls were being kept." Dallas glanced out the window as the private jet whizzed through thick clouds. "He kept meticulous records of the finances, even of those who paid in cryptocurrency. This racket was farther reaching than anyone suspected."

"Were all the girls found…alive?" Alicia asked in a whisper.

Dallas' expression turned somber, as a tear formed in the corner of his left eye. "Not all of them. Sadly, the girls shared which had been killed."

Alicia made the sign of the cross and whispered a prayer for their souls.

"It's insane to think someone would go to such lengths," Dallas pounded his thigh. "When I first heard of my card being cloned, I was pissed off."

"And rightfully so," she added.

"When we learned of the girls going missing, and things changed." His head swayed from side to side. "My money was no longer my focus. My thoughts immediately went to the girls and their families."

Alicia placed warm palms alongside his face, "As you've said. Human trafficking is a multi-billion-dollar industry. There's no way to know how far corruption has spread."

"Uncovering these bastards put a serious dent in things. From lawyers to judges, politicians to pediatricians, Shahid spilled his guts."

Alicia massaged her temples with her forefinger and thumb. "He must have gotten a pretty good deal to turn on such powerful individuals."

"I am certain he thought he did. But with the death of children, he is going to serve time." Dallas exhaled deeply. "I guess all we can hope for is to do what we can …."

"With what we have…where we are," she said.

Heidi returned with Alicia's water. "What do you think will happen to her?" she tilted her head in Zoe's direction.

"Something tells me she's a fighter," he said. "If she turns out to be anything like you, she is going to be just fine."

"When we get back to your condo, I'm going to unpack, and not even think about suitcases for a very long time," she said, snuggling up to his chest.

"I'm going to hold you to it," he said.

"Please do."

 Epilogue

An immediate hush filled the room as she entered the stage and stepped towards the podium. Her white, silk, button down blouse was a perfect match for the wide-legged high-waisted charcoal slacks. A single strand of pearls circled her neck. Her thick auburn hair pulled up into a messy bun. Diamond teardrop earring graced each lob.

As she stood overlooking the masses, she couldn't believe this was her life. From the moment she was able to walk, she knew life had given her a purpose. She never could've imagined it would bring her here. Darkness once gripped her in fear, but today, both bowed down. This was her pulpit. The masses were her parishioners. Delivering those trapped in a web of deceit was her mission.

Taking a sip of sparkling water from the bottle beside the microphone she said, "Hello and thank you for coming. My name's Zoe and I'm the COO of A Place to Ponder. I'm also a survivor of human trafficking." She squared her shoulders and leveled her head. "Make that I'm a thriver."

Chairs scraped against the marble floor as individuals gave a standing ovation.

"I want to share my journey from that of being a victim to a victor and share how I advocated for the very laws that placed my abductor behind bars. And not just him," she said. "But everyone that collaborated with him to prosper for the trafficking of young lives.

"Tonight, I'll share how you can join A Place to Ponder in our fight against those who prey upon our most vulnerable citizens."

Excerpt from Queen of Belize by Aiken Ponder

Prologue

"Don't kill her," he begged as his hands went up, and the unmistakable stench of fear permeated the air. "Please … let me live."

Robert's eyes bulged to the point of nearly popping out of the sockets and ricocheting across the living room floor. His amber skin was ashen with terror. "You don't have to do this."

With each tearful plea, he inched ever so slightly to the left.

"Do you really think I'm that stupid?" Her lips curled over her upper teeth. Within nanoseconds, she was in his face spitting out each word. Dirty fingernails chewed down to nubs gripped the handle of the M5. "I know what you're trying to do."

Ironically, the weapon had been a Christmas gift from him.

The thought that he once loved the demon in a meat-suit now standing before him, masquerading as a human, caused bile to rise in the back of his throat and nearly choke him.

How could someone who'd once taken his breath away now want to end his life?

"I know what you're doing." She instantly became judge and jury of his actions. "Dumb ass. I helped you to retrofit the curio to hold the weapons."

She kicked several empty moving boxes out of the way as she stomped over and yanked open the top drawer. "Ah, the .38 Special on steroids. It's still loaded just like I left it." She thrust the Smith and Wesson .357 Magnum revolver into her belted waistband. "You won't be needing this."

Robert immediately dropped to his knees, laced his fingers together, and swayed from side to side trying to contain the excruciating emotional pain. "Why're you doing this?" His throat was on fire. Vocal cords felt as though they were being sliced with a white-hot sword. At that moment, he didn't exude the swagger that accompanied being the youngest Black attorney with Appleman, Greenhagen, and Einhorn, LLP; Robert sounded like a television commercial that warned about the dangers of nicotine. "You already killed my father," he moaned.

"Daddy," Ivy Davidson bellowed over her shoulder, loud enough for her voice to carry into the adjacent room. "Show the good attorney that we mean business with his lady friend."

Rahul Perez's soiled, steel-toe boots trudged along the hand-scraped teakwood floors. Heavy steps left thick, black scuff marks in his path.

Bam! The bathroom door splintered as it flew completely off the hinges. It bounced against the wall and shattered on the floor removing the sole source of protection for his new bride.

Robert collapsed to the rug, protesting, "She never did anything to you. Please don't take this out on her. Our marriage was over long before—"

"Before what?" she seethed. "Before you tried to steal my babies? Or when you left me homeless?" Ivy jammed the barrel of the gun so deeply into his left temple, droplets of blood dripped down his face and onto the collar of the linen shirt, instantly turning the white fabric bright red.

He leaped to his feet and lunged at her, attempting to snatch the weapon but lost his footing. His chin smacked against the floor as he went face down. Ivy struck his head with such force, his teeth rattled. The droplets of blood became a river and gushed uncontrollably. His left eye swelled shut, and his head began to pound.

Urine drenched his organic cotton khaki shorts, saturating the hand-woven Persian rug.

Her nose wrinkled as she sniffed. "Daddy," she shouted. "The son of a bitch pissed himself." Her laughter was maniacal. "I should kill you right now but witnessing your pain is so much sweeter." She stooped and stared him in the eye. "And, trust me, you will lose everything!"

She whispered in his ear, "Where are my manners?" Her hot, putrid breath invaded his nostrils. "You shouldn't be having all this fun without your fiancé, now, should you?"

She shouted into the next room, "Kick her in the face, Daddy."

Blood-curdling screams reverberated throughout the spacious rooms and bounced off priceless African artifacts. In a previous life, the statues had witnessed unspeakable carnage. Robert brought the relics home from his many excursions in hope that they'd find solace. He had freed them, but who was going to rescue him?

The faint sound of police sirens rang in the distance. "Dammit, Daddy! Get it over with." A string of saliva defied gravity as it dribbled off her chin. "Just put a bullet to the back of her head."

Rahul Perez pulled the trigger of the Glock 19 and fired just as the Westminster Quarters in the grandfather clock marked seven o'clock. Robert's screams exploded from a place so deep within his soul that his heart shattered into a thousand pieces.

"You are next," Ivy warned.

Robert looked up through tears as the bright light of the muzzle flashed nanoseconds before the bullet ripped through his chest. He never saw the second, third, or fourth shot. Robert Davidson fell dead on the floor he had laid with his own hands.

About the book:

By birth, she is royalty. By choice she is an avenger and equalizer for those who have no voice. When dark forces emerge and threaten not only her queendom but her life, Luiza, Queen of Belize becomes a foot soldier, calling upon the assistance of allies and a few nemeses to help aid in a personal war. It's then that she fulfills the meaning of her name, glorious war hero.

PURPOSE

Life According to God's Plan

FLORENZA DENISE LEE

Excerpt from Purpose

Sixteen Years Old - 1980

"Suicide hotline, please hold."

If music played or if I stood there in silence, I cannot recall. What I do remember is my shaking hand cradling the receiver to my ear. The click of being placed on hold was the loudest sound I'd ever heard. I was in total disbelief. To this day, reflecting on that pivotal moment causes my skin to crawl. My vision blurred, then tunneled as my mind spun like a roulette wheel—around and round, it went. Holding my breath, I waited for the little white ball to stop. Secretly, I feared I was about to create a new landing space. If this proved to be accurate, I worried I would not survive.

The plush tan carpet found its way between blue-painted toes as my bare feet teetered on the edge of the first step on the landing. With sweaty palms, I gripped the handrail, fearing my knees might give way as I felt the cream-colored walls pressing in. Finding my voice, and it shook with fear. "Hello, is anyone there?"

Tears stung my eyes as I realized my lifeline had failed me. Yet again, I was left alone.

Fine. If I can't get help, I'll just do it.

It's surprising how determination manifests at the most inopportune time. Just moments prior, I'd lacked the strength to hold a phone to my ear. Yet now, I felt I could lift a car. I punched the disconnect button to end the call and stretched my five-foot three-inch frame as I reasoned within myself. Perhaps they were counseling some other soul who needed assistance. I prayed they'd at least received what I hadn't.

Phone in hand, I counted the eight steps back to the only bathroom in our three-bedroom home. Some might consider it a small house, but to us, it was a palace. Glancing to my right, I saw my brother's bedroom. He was the only boy and always had his own space. For a moment, I thought about tidying it for him but decided otherwise—no time to spare. I was on a mission.

The bedroom that I shared with my two sisters was just a few feet away. Bunkbeds flanked the far wall. A twin-size bed was parallel to it. Bed linen, curtains, throw rugs—nothing matched.

Without even looking underneath the single bed, I knew what was there, well-read books, and many. Each night, I read by the streetlight that flooded through the small window. If I had five cents for every time my mother caught me reading past bedtime, let's just say I'd have a lot of nickels. I'm going to miss my books the most.

I could not silence the woman's voice as it screamed, please hold inside my head, mocking my pain. What I interpreted from her actions was, "Who are you trying to fool? You aren't about to do anything irrational. Stop wasting my time."

"Oh, I'm not, am I? Then watch this." Stomping to the bathroom, I retrieved several bottles from the metal shelves and then lined the contents along the edge of the white porcelain sink. The thought to flush them down the toilet or wash them down the drain left as fast as it entered my mind. Overtaking me was a determination to be destructive.

When they find out I was serious, I bet they'll never place another caller on hold.

If the camel needed a straw to break its back, a call on hold was it.

About the Author

Aiken Ponder grew up admiring authors that wielded their pens like a sword. Learning from the masters, she too put pen to paper, clearing her path to success. Aiken writes across many genres, including Erotica, Mysteries, Paranormal, and Adult Contemporary Literature.

Aiken is a member of NK Tribe called Success and Cavalcade of Authors. Her debut book, 80 Days of Pleasure, collaborates with New York Times and USA Today Bestselling Authors. Aiken's books feature powerful women who unapologetically embrace their authenticity and boldly walk in their purpose and passion.

You may follow her on all social media sites under Aiken Ponder.

IG: https://www.instagram.com/aiken_ponder/

Facebook: https://www.facebook.com/AuthorAikenPonder/

Website: www.aikenponder.com

I am so thankful for your support and look forward to reading your reviews.

About the Days of Pleasure Series
9 Books * All Standalones * No Cliffhangers

10 Days of Pleasure

Some relationships are made in the storm. Real love survives them. Basketball star Dallas Avery has the world in the palm of his hand and a lifetime of happiness or despair within his grasp. For accomplished businesswoman, Alicia Mitchell, love is a double-edged sword wrought with happiness and pain. Business calls the soulmates to Scotland but a new, more treacherous storm is brewing back home. Can their love weather this latest test, or will a crueler fate prevail?

20 Days of Pleasure

NBA star Dallas Avery has one intention when he visits the most romantic city in the world—win Alicia Mitchell by any means necessary. They relish their time as a couple—free to explore their magnetic connection in Paris and savor the array of pleasures they discover as soul mates.

But family, friends, the media, and society at large, have various opinions about their complicated relationship. Will Dallas and Alicia find a way to stay together, or will the many factors working against them shatter their once-in-a-lifetime romance?

30 Days of Pleasure

Every end is supposed to be a beginning. After the death of her husband, Alicia Mitchell set herself up financially to embrace freedom and see the world. Then she met a detour. Until NBA basketball star Dallas Avery wrapped his arms around her, Alicia didn't know what it felt like to be cherished. Now he's drawing her focus and shifting her priorities. And Alicia doesn't mind. However, there's a shadow creeping from the edges of her dating history.

Taric Hasan, a man she considered dating until she experienced his dark side, has emerged. Although she once managed to escape him, Taric isn't done with her. He's intent on ending their relationship on his terms … with her death.

40 Days of Pleasure

The NBA's sexy and most valuable player Dallas Avery meets the beautiful Alicia Mitchell, who has one thing on her mind: leaving. Their attraction is intense, but the timing is off. Dallas is determined to convince Alicia to give their May-December relationship a chance, but when their romantic trip to the Caribbean gets derailed by them being embroiled in a local family's deadly drama, romance gets put on the back burner.

50 Days of Pleasure

When an obsessive fan threatens to derail Basketball Superstar Dallas Avery's relationship with the alluring and independent Alicia Mitchell, a trip to Canada comes at the opportune time. The historic sites and chilly landscapes help to stir the growing connection between the couple.

Then a distressed infant is thrust into their care. The teenage mother and her baby are in danger and only trust Dallas and Alicia to help. With the local mob in pursuit and Dallas and Alicia unable to depend on the police, they must flee the country using a historic mode of escape.

60 Days of Pleasure

Determined to give Alicia Mitchell the love that she longs for, NBA-star Dallas Avery whisks her away on exciting adventures around the world.

Dallas let his heart dictate their journey to Seattle and allows the Emerald City to work its magic on Alicia. Until civil unrest involving the indigenous people collides with a dirty politician's plans to use city funds to cover personal debts. A chance meeting with Yuma, a tribal chief's son, creates an opportunity for Dallas to make a difference for those whose voices have been silenced. When an altercation with the police develops after Dallas and Alicia assist a homeless woman, Yuma's tribe is forced to shift gears and protect the couple.

Can Dallas keep the love of his life safe, and will the civil unrest drive a permanent wedge between them?

70 Days of Pleasure

Dallas Avery and Alicia Mitchell are off to Nashville, Tennessee for business and pleasure. Unfortunately, the past returns to haunt the basketball superstar and puts both in imminent danger.

Conway Ackerman has spent the last five years in prison, charged with aggravated stalking of the athlete early in his career. A bitter man with a sordid past, and a psychotic personality, Ackerman has recently been let out of prison and has set a course that will exact the perfect revenge.

While Dallas is aware of the convict's release, he keeps Alicia in the dark. The stage is set for a myriad of adventures, which will extend to the iconic Beale Street in Memphis, but danger is in the midst. A race against time ensues as the couple is tracked from place to place. Will they survive or meet their demise at the hands of a man whose mental state is deadly?

80 Days of Pleasure

From a romantic picnic in the Southwest to jet-setting around the globe to exotic destinations, Dallas Avery lays the foundation for a long-lasting relationship with Alicia Mitchell, brick by brick, beginning with these five words, "Just one more day, baby."

While traveling the romantic countryside from Munich, Germany to Schloss Neuschwanstein, a case of mistaken identity threatens their freedom and possibly their lives. Dallas has faced numerous threats, but nothing could have prepared him for this experience. A desire to make Alicia's childhood dream come true has evolved into an incredible nightmare.

Dallas and Alicia struggle to learn the new rules of engagement they have been forced to play by. One thing is certain, the NBA player is determined they will not be on the losing end.

90 Days of Pleasure

Alicia Mitchell, is and was, the only woman Dallas Avery has ever loved. He strives to soothe her fears about their age difference, the unresolved issues of her past, and is determined to make her his forever.

An impromptu trip to Durabia brings more danger to their relationship. Crown Prince Amir sets his sights on Alicia and puts a diabolical plan in motion for her to be secretly brought into the palace where he can have her all to himself. None of them could fathom that a third party would intervene, and plunge Dallas and Alicia in the middle of a brotherly war.

USA TODAY Bestselling Author, Naleighna Kai, tells the dynamic love triangle of a chance encounter that lands wealthy NBA star, Dallas Avery, back in the arms of Alicia, the woman of his dreams. A woman he hasn't seen in years. A woman he soon discovers is his fiancée's long-lost aunt!

But Tori, isn't ready to give up all that she's worked for in their relationship, so she makes him a shocking offer—go through with the wedding and she'll still allow him to be with the one woman he now can't seem to do without. Dallas will get a family, something her aunt can't give him and Tori will have the lifestyle she clamors. And Alicia will embrace the love she's longed for all her life and that had already been in her reach before she disappeared. Everyone will get a little of what they want. . . and maybe a whole lot of what they don't.

The details of the trio's love life play out in the tabloids and on talk shows, making Dallas the center of an NBA scandal. Eventually, the doors slam shut on this open marriage in the making and Dallas is forced to make a choice to end the chaos.

Dallas & Alicia's Story Continues in Open Door Marriage

```
Three years later . . .
```

Thanksgiving - Chicago, Illinois
November 22—7:23 p.m.

"You slept with my aunt?"

The words still didn't register, even though this had to be Tori's fifth time saying them. She glared at her fiancé, still desperately trying to come to terms with the information her mother had blasted to everyone at the packed Thanksgiving dinner table.

"Seriously? How is that even humanly possible when you didn't know the woman four hours ago?" Tori shouted.

"Tori, l-let me explain," Dallas stammered.

Twelve pairs of eyes were now focused on the not-quite-blissful couple standing at the bottom of the stairs just off from the dining room.

"But not here. Let's go somewhere and talk. It's not what you think."

"What did you do?" Tori snapped, glaring up at him. "Trip over the sheets, and your penis somehow landed in a woman nearly twice my age?"

The drumstick in Uncle Bill's hand paused in midair on its journey to his wide mouth. Cousin Tiny's fleshy hand flew to her overexposed bosom and came to rest somewhere above her heart. Even her father's frozen expression of alarm would have been Three Stooges comical if the situation weren't so tragic.

Aunt Yoli was the first to recover. "Did she just say what I think she said?"

In unison, everyone nodded.

"Girl, shut the front door and run out the back!"

A few bursts of nervous laughter sprang up around the table, but they were not nearly enough to chase away the unease that had flooded the room when Tori stepped into the house. She'd gone to drop off Aunt Rose's drunk self at home. Tori hadn't even been in the house good when her mother, Bernice, blurted out that she'd caught Alicia and Dallas together. Alone. In bed. In the nude. Tori had picked up from there and summed it up in one sweep. "You slept with my aunt ..."

"Nothing happened," Dallas said, his voice solid. "I didn't sleep with her."

"So, my mama's lying?" Tori asked.

Dallas shifted uneasily.

"Hell naw. I know what I saw," Bernice snapped. She had moved from the dining room table to the end of the staircase, right next to her daughter, poised as if she was ready to go to battle. "Both of you were in bed butt-ass naked." She jabbed a finger in her sister-in-law's direction. Alicia hadn't moved from her spot at the top of the staircase. Probably, because she knew what was best for her. "She was butt-naked. And he was nut-naked," Bernice yelled. "Wasn't an inch of space between them." She flickered a gaze at Dallas. "Look at him. You can tell he just got dressed."

Tori closed her eyes and took deep breaths to calm the emotions that warred within her.

"See, I told you Alicia wasn't worth a damn," Bernice crowed with savage satisfaction. "And looks like Mr. NBA ain't much better. You thought he was all that and a side order of fries."

Dallas Avery was the NBA's most valuable player, and a man most women would give their right and left ovary to call their own. But Most Eligible Bachelor or not, he had set Tori's bitch meter into overdrive. Even with his chiseled, handsome face, towering muscular frame, and million dollar bank accounts, he was now worth next to nothing in her eyes. Too bad her aching heart didn't get that memo.

Tori didn't know if she was more enraged or hurt that her mother had been all too willing to drive this stake through her own daughter's heart in order to publicly disgrace Alicia.

"We need to talk about this," Dallas repeated before adding, "in private."

Bernice wore a satisfied smirk as she glared openly up at Alicia, who just kept staring stoically at them from the second floor landing. "The angel of the family has fallen," Bernice said.

"Hey, Bernice," Bill taunted with a hearty chuckle. "Bet you won't say that when Alicia comes downstairs. You know she's gonna put a hurting on you."

"You mean put *another* hurting on her," Aunt Yoli added, doubling over with laughter.

Tori wanted to scream. Her life was unraveling in front of her, and her family was cracking jokes.

Instinctively, Bernice inched away from the staircase and back toward the dining room table. Her hands went up to the scar on her neck, probably remembering that a year ago on this very same holiday, Alicia had ended a vicious blow-for-blow fight with a knife at Bernice's throat. Almost gave the woman a "Sicilian Smile"—an ear-to-ear slice across the throat.

Dallas reached for Tori's hand. "It's not what it seems."

She snatched away, parted her lips to give him what was left of her mind, but Cousin Tiny chimed in first. "Alicia had every right to take Bernice to the floor last year for that foul mess she said. I would've pulled out my own can of whoop ass behind that one."

Tiny's husband, Thomas, nodded his watermelon-sized head.

The rest of the family finally sprang to life, also chiming in at once to defend Alicia, the one woman everyone could count on in a time of need, to lend an ear when it was called for and to dry a tear when no one else bothered to care. That she would do something as low as sleep with her niece's soon-to-be husband was unthinkable. So the family sidestepped that issue for as long as they could, finding it more comfortable to speak on the reason no one had expected Alicia home for Thanksgiving—especially since none of them had heard from her for an entire year.

Dallas maneuvered so he was in front of Tori. "Nothing. Happened."

"If Bernice had said that bull to me," Bill responded, still trying to tackle the last of the drumstick, "an ass whipping would've been the least of her problems." He beckoned toward the last slice of sweet potato pie at the other end of the table. "That has my name written all over it."

"Bernice is lying," Martha said. "Alicia's still got looks and all, but that young stud wouldn't pick her over Tori." She shot an appreciative glance toward Dallas, then leaned to her right and whispered loudly in Yoli's direction, "But, girl, he is finer than frog's hair."

Yoli gave him a lusty once-over. "I'd give him some my damn self. He's the type of man who can make a woman put a for sale sign on one thigh and an open for business sign on the other. Yes, Lawd."

Tori tried her best to tune out her family. She didn't have the stamina to deal with them right now. "How could you do this? You're my fiancé."

"You're Tori's fiancé?" Alicia finally spoke out. She eased down the stairs, looking first to Tori then to Dallas. Her panic-stricken expression gave Tori pause. Could her aunt really have not known?

Alicia turned back to her niece. "Oh, my, God, Tori. I had no idea. I'm so, so sorry." She didn't give Tori time to reply as she brushed past Dallas, slipped into the nearest pair of shoes—her brother's—and ran out of the front door, oblivious to the fact that she barely had on enough clothing to protect her from the chill in the room, let alone the sub-zero temps of a Chicago winter.

The whole crowd gasped in disbelief as Dallas grabbed his leather coat from the foyer closet. "She can't go out there with nothing on," he said as he stepped into his Timberlands. "I'll be right back."

Tori was ready to spit fire. "Are you kidding me?" she screamed as he quickly laced up his shoes, then darted toward the door. "You're going after my aunt? My aunt," she yelled, following him. "My heart is bleeding all over the carpet and you're going after *her*."

The front door slammed, and Tori stood frozen, unable to believe what happened in the last ten minutes. Bernice's voice snapped Tori out of her trance. "Girl, I taught you better than that," Bernice yelled, gesturing to the door. "You'd better go get your man."

Tori snatched up a coat and scarf and braced herself against the frigid gust of wind that slapped her as she left the house. She trekked across the snow and barely reached Dallas before he pulled off. Banging on the glass, she demanded, "Where the hell are you going?"

Dallas lowered the window. "She's out there unprotected. None of this is her fault."

"So now you're speaking up for her, too?" Tori screeched, pummeling him through the opening. "What kind of bullshit is that?"

Dallas flinched at her vicious tone and reached out to keep her hands from doing any more damage. "I'm going to say two things," he replied in that businesslike tone that had landed him several million-dollar endorsement deals. "I'm sorry that your mother lied to you, but nothing happened." His gaze swept the area, probably searching for the woman who was the center of the chaos. "And I'd be less of a man than you already think I am if I let that woman walk around in this weather without a coat."

Tori gave his words a moment's consideration. Causing a scene wouldn't stop him from doing what he felt he had to do, so she made a dash for the passenger side. "I'm coming with you."

They caught up with Alicia at the end of Harper Avenue, where she made a left and was now struggling up the path a block away from the main thoroughfare. She was shaking uncontrollably from the cold and from the sobs that wracked her body.

"Get in, Alicia," Dallas commanded, trailing the distraught woman as she stumbled along the icy sidewalk in shoes that were three sizes too big.

Alicia covered her mouth as though to keep in the words that threatened to spill out. She continued forward, wavering while trying to balance in the oversized loafers on snow that came up to her calves on unshoveled parts of the sidewalk.

"Don't make me get out of the car," Dallas said through his teeth.

Alicia ignored the threat, forcing the car to continue following her until she made it to a glass bus shelter on Stony Island Avenue. She swept the snow away from the steel bench, crawled on it, then tucked her legs up under her as though preparing to spend the night.

Dallas was out of the car and by her side in the time it took to blink. He whipped off his leather coat, placed it about Alicia's shoulders, then held out his hand to her. It took a moment for her to take it, but finally she stood. Together, they took two steps, then, she crumbled down onto the snow.

"Ouch," she shrieked. "My ankle."

It took Dallas only a moment to lift her into his arms, then navigate carefully over the slick pavement. He placed her gently, almost lovingly, in the back seat of his rented Benz. Using the sleeve of his shirt, he wiped her tears away.

Tori felt like she was having an out-of-body experience. The way Dallas looked at Alicia. The way he held her. It tore at Tori's gut. "Dallas, what's going on?" Tori asked once he was back in the driver's seat. "How the hell have you connected with her in such a way that you feel obligated to ease her pain and not mine?" The anger was still there, but Tori tried to push it aside, because right now, she needed clarity.

Dallas carefully pulled onto the street and aimed the car back in the direction of the place they'd just left. "We'll talk about this when we get back to the house."

"No," Alicia cried out, gripping the edge of the driver's seat and causing Dallas to punch the brakes. "I can't go back there. Not right now."

Dallas locked gazes with her in the rear view mirror. "Where do you want me to take you?"

"I don't know. Anywhere but there," she whispered, slumping back down in the seat. "Anywhere but home." Alicia's shoulders shook with an effort to hold herself together, and Dallas' expression softened.

The whole scenario made Tori's heart constrict as though someone had put a vise grip on the very thing that kept her alive.

She had only been gone for three hours. What the hell had happened between Dallas and her aunt?